THE BOOK OF
TOYTOWN
AND LARRY THE LAMB

THE BOOK OF
TOYTOWN
AND LARRY THE LAMB

Written and Illustrated by
S.G. HULME BEAMAN

With a biographical note
about the author
by HENDRIK BAKER

Harrap   London

This edition first published in Great Britain 1979
by GEORGE G. HARRAP & CO. LTD
182 High Holborn, London WC1V 7AX

Reprinted: 1980

Stories and illustrations © *Larry the Lamb Ltd* 1979
Biographical note about the Author © *Hendrik Baker* 1979

ISBN 0 245 53457 1

Designed by Michael R. Carter

Made in Great Britain
Printed by Martin's Printing Works, Berwick upon Tweed
Bound by Western Book Company, Maesteg

Contents

Colour Plates

Publisher's Note

In 1928 the B.B.C. broadcast the first Toytown story in Children's Hour. From then until the B.B.C. closed down Children's Hour in 1963 the Toytown stories were its most popular feature; yet the author, S. G. Hulme Beaman, only wrote twenty-eight episodes for radio before he died in 1932. These, and some other stories, appeared in book form, and since the inauguration of television Toytown and its best known character, Larry the Lamb, have appeared in various adaptations for that medium. The colour plates in this book are taken from the television films.

In this volume, produced with the approval of the author's family, his friend Hendrik Baker has selected seven stories and illustrations which convey the essence of the appeal of Toytown and he has also added a biographical sketch of the author, whose name must surely rank alongside the greatest of those who have provided literary and dramatic entertainment for children. We are proud to be associated with this unique project.

The Road to Toytown

TOM had heard that Toytown was a very wonderful place. He was so anxious to see it that one day he decided to set out to find it.

'Trot,' he said to his dog, 'how would you like to come with me and have some adventures?'

'What sort of adventures?' Trot asked.

'We might have all sorts of adventures,' Tom replied. 'When boys and dogs go to seek their fortunes, there is no knowing what may happen to them. I'm going to Toytown, if I can find it.'

'Is it very far?' Trot asked.

'I don't know,' said Tom. 'I have heard that if you walk over those hills and through the forest, and keep walking, you will come to Toytown at last. But I believe there are dragons in the forest, and fairies, and all sorts of things. So we should have plenty of adventures.'

'Do dragons eat puppies?' asked Trot.

'I believe that dragons are very fond of dogs,' Tom told him. 'But of course, if you are afraid, you had better stay at home.'

'Who's afraid?' cried Trot. 'I'm a very brave little dog really. But I am wondering whether we should get plenty to eat on the journey. I should hate to go without bones. Besides, we might get lost.'

But Tom made him see what fine fun it would be to steal away over the hills in search of adventures; and at last Trot agreed to go with him.

So early next morning, before any one else was about, they made a bundle of a clean collar, some cakes, and a bone for Trot, and set out. Tom carried the bundle on a stick over his shoulder, for, he said, every one who goes to seek his fortune carries a bundle on a stick. Up the hills they went. Trot gambolled along in front, and Tom followed. Although they went quite fast, it was a long time before they reached the top of the highest hill.

The two friends sat down and ate some of their cakes, for they were feeling very tired. Trot wanted to go to sleep, but Tom would not let him, and prodded him every now and again with his stick. This made Trot very angry.

'You can't go to sleep yet,' Tom told him. 'We have a long way to go.'

And he got to his feet and led the way down the hill towards the forest, which they could just see in the distance.

They had not gone very far before they saw an old gentleman coming towards them. Tom ran up to him and bowed politely.

'Please, sir,' said he, 'can you tell me whether we are on the right road for Toytown?'

The old gentleman looked surprised.

'Are you going all the way to Toytown?' he asked.

'Yes sir, if we can find it,' Tom replied.

'Well,' said the old gentleman, 'it is not very far, but the trouble is that the forest is said to be full of dragons and wizards and things; not at all safe for little boys. But if you must go, keep straight on through the forest.'

Tom thanked him, and set off again, followed by Trot, and it was not very long before they found themselves entering the forest. Then Trot began to wish he had not come; the forest was so very dark, and he expected every moment to be pounced upon by a dragon.

'I'm not sure I should have come with you', he said to Tom at last. 'I've been thinking hard ever since we started, and I am afraid it was wrong of me to leave home. You see, there is no one to mind the house, or to bark when strangers come near it. I really think I ought to turn back.'

'Nonsense!' cried Tom. 'Mind the house, indeed! Why, if any stranger did come near, you would be asleep in your kennel. *I* have never heard you bark except when you wanted something to eat.'

'That is what I'm troubled about,' Trot said; 'I might have been a better dog.'

'You're afraid,' his friend told him. 'That's what your trouble is. Come along—be brave.'

So Trot had to follow Tom; but every few moments he looked around to see if there were any dragons about. At last, through not looking where he was going, he bumped his nose very hard against a tree, and sat down to rub it with his paw. But he soon forgot his hurt when Tom suddenly shouted, 'Look! a house!' And, sure enough, there in front was a little house among the trees.

11

'Now we shall be able to rest and have something nice to eat,' Tom said, and he led the way towards the house.

As they drew near it, the door opened, and a very old woman came hobbling out on a stick. Tom felt a little afraid when he saw her; he thought of witches. But now it was Trot who was eager to go ahead, for he could smell something cooking inside the cottage.

'How are you, my little lad?' the old woman asked. 'Won't you step inside my cottage and rest?'

Tom took off his hat politely, and followed her into the house, with Trot close upon his heels. It was really a dear little house, full of quaint furniture, with a large black cat asleep before the fire. Trot waggled his ears when he saw the cat. But as it only blinked lazily at him and did not spring up to fight him, Trot began wondering about the pot over the fire, from which the nice smell was coming.

The old lady gave them a very good dinner, but the more Tom looked at her, the more anxious he became.

'I'm sure she is a witch,' he whispered to Trot, 'and if she is, we must escape before she eats us or turns us into nasty animals. Look!' he added, 'I can see a broomstick in that corner.'

'It isn't only witches who have broomsticks,' Trot muttered. He was feeling very warm and comfortable, and did not want to be disturbed.

Then, as the old woman went out of the room, Tom whispered, 'I have an idea Trot. If she *is* a witch, that will be a magic broomstick, and every one (except puppies) knows that if you get on a magic broomstick and wish hard, it will fly up into the air with you. Let's try it.'

'I'm very tired,' Trot muttered, closing his eyes. 'Do leave me alone.'

But Tom would have his way. He made Trot get up. Then, tiptoeing across the room, he seized the broomstick and rushed

out of the house.

The old woman, however, had heard him, and came running after, shouting, 'Bring back my broomstick! Bring back my broomstick!'

'Quick!' said Tom. He sat astride the broom, and dragged Trot in front of him. 'Wish hard.'

'I wish I could have another helping of meat,' Trot muttered.

'No,' cried Tom; 'I mean, wish we were up in the air. Now, both together. Wish hard.'

They both wished, and the broomstick shot up into the air like a bird, carrying Tom and Trot with it; and the old woman looked up at them and danced with rage at seeing her magic broomstick taken from her.

Higher and higher went the two friends, until Trot began to feel very much afraid.

'How can we stop it?' he asked. 'If this nasty broom goes much higher we shall hit the moon. And if we wish suddenly to be down again it will let us down with a terrible bump.'

'I know,' Tom cried. 'We must wish where we want to go.'

13

'I want to go home,' said Trot; and as soon as he had said it, the broomstick began to wobble.

'No, no,' Tom said; 'we don't want to go home. We want to go to Toytown. We must wish the broomstick to take us to Toytown. Now, wish hard.'

'What I really wish——' began Trot.

But Tom prodded him angrily, and Trot wished properly. At once the broomstick sailed round in a circle, and began to fly away over the trees; indeed, it went so fast that Tom had to hold his hat in case it blew away, and Trot blinked his eyes, which were full of water.

'This is better than walking,' Tom shouted in Trot's ear.

'Yes,' Trot agreed, 'it's better than walking, but I do wish——'

'Don't wish anything,' cried Tom; 'wait until we reach Toytown. Then you can wish whatever you like.'

So it was on the magic broomstick that Tom and Trot reached Toytown, and Tom thought they were very lucky to have saved so much time. It would have taken days to walk, but the broomstick got them there in five minutes. It sailed up to the walls of the Town, circled round, and dropped gently to the ground in front of the gate.

Tom and Trot jumped off, and Trot cried angrily, 'I wish that nasty broomstick would go home.' At once the broom rose in the air, and sailed away.

In front of the gate of Toytown stood a sentry, and he stared very hard as the two friends came up to him. He was not used to seeing people ride about on broomsticks. However, he saluted quite politely when Tom raised his hat and asked if he and Trot might go in.

'Dogs are not admitted,' the soldier replied.

'Oh, but sir,' cried Tom, 'we have come a terribly long way, and I can't leave my little dog outside.'

'Certainly not,' added Trot.

14

'DOGS—ARE—NOT—ADMITTED,' repeated the sentry sternly.

'Oh, what ever shall we do?' cried Tom.

'Except on a lead,' the soldier said, after a pause. 'Now, if your little dog was on a lead I could let him in.'

'But we haven't a lead,' Tom explained.

'Then he can't come in,' the soldier said. He seemed to think hard for a moment. 'Of course, a piece of string would do.'

'Oh, could you lend me a piece of string?' begged Tom.

The soldier thought again. 'Of course I could,' he said, 'but I'm on duty. Sentries on duty are not allowed to let go of their rifles to take pieces of string out of their pockets.'

'Then, please let me feel in your pocket for some string,' said Tom.

'Very well,' replied the sentry. 'I do not mind that. I know there is a piece of string in my pocket, because I had a piece to mend my belt with. But be careful not to tickle me, because I might drop my rifle. Then I should get into trouble.'

Tom felt very carefully in the soldier's pocket, and was much pleased to find a long piece of string. It was true that it had many knots in it, but this did not matter. He tied one end round Trot's neck and held the other in his hand. The sentry examined the string very carefully, to see that it was properly tied; then he threw open the gate, and saluted Tom and Trot as they passed inside.

So our two little friends came safely to Toytown, which they found was indeed a very wonderful place. It would take a long time to tell you of all the strange things they saw and heard, but some of the best known stories about Toytown are those that come next.

Going to the Fair

I

THREE small animals sat on a door-step in Golliwog Lane, Toytown, and stared dolefully at a row of pennies arranged in front of them. They were Larry the lamb, Toby the white dog, and Dennis the dachshund.

'This is dreadful!' said Larry. 'I'm sure there is not enough there to pay all our fares to Arkville!'

'So one of us won't be able to go,' observed Toby.

'And I know which one that will be,' said Larry. 'Me! You two dogs always take advantage of me, just because I'm a little lamb. And I wanted very much to see the fair at Arkville!'

'Possibly no doubt the coach-fares for this great occasion reduced have been,' Dennis suggested. 'Therefore would it not be well at the coach-office to enquire?'

'Oh yes, Dennis; you go and ask,' Larry said. 'They'll pay more attention to you; nobody takes any notice of lambs.'

16

Dennis left his two friends to guard the money, and trotted off towards the Arkville Gate, where the coach-office was. The driver (who acted as ticket-clerk in his spare time) was seated inside, and Dennis peered cautiously round the door and spoke to him.

'Please excuse, Herr Driver,' he said, 'but how much is the fare to Arkville to-morrow?'

'Same as it always is,' replied the driver. 'We're not charging any more on account of the fair. Ninepence each, and sixpence for children and animals. Passengers' luggage carried free.'

'Thank you; most grateful I am,' said Dennis politely. 'A lovely day it has become, no doubt, perhaps?'

'The same to you,' replied the coach-driver. Dennis returned to his friends looking very thoughtful.

'Sixpence each, the fare is,' he told them.

'Oh Dennis, and we have only one and two-pence!' cried Larry. 'One of us will have to stop at home.'

'Not so, Larry, my friend,' said Dennis. 'For an idea I have most excellent.' Looking cautiously around, he bent forward and whispered behind his paw: 'The luggage of passengers is free!'

II

The next morning the coach stood in the open space before the Arkville Gate, ready to make the daily journey to Arkville. One or two persons had already taken their seats when Dennis and Toby hurried round the corner and went up to the driver, who was chatting with the guard.

'Oh, Mr. Driver, is this right for Arkville?' Toby asked. 'Because if so, my friend Dennis and I would like to go. And please, can we have front seats?'

'Have you got any money?' the driver asked, looking hard at him.

For an answer Toby unclasped his paw and showed the driver two sixpences. 'And we are taking some luggage with us,' he said. 'Would you and Mr. Guard be so kind as to help us with it? Because we are two very small animals and we can't manage it alone. It's just round the corner on the kerb.'

The driver and the guard followed the animals into Golliwog Lane, and there, resting on the kerb, was a large packing-case.

'This no doubt our luggage was, very likely,' said Dennis.

'I never did hear anyone talk so funny as what you do!' exclaimed the driver. 'Is it your luggage, or isn't it?'

'It is, Herr Guard,' replied Dennis. 'Therefore please most carefully to lift it, the contents being most extremely fragile.'

'They're most extremely heavy,' said the guard, as he and his companion lifted the case. 'What's inside?'

'Things extremely personal,' replied Dennis. 'Right side up please convey it.'

The guard and the driver carried the case to the coach, and had hoisted it onto the roof, when the Magician hurried round the corner. He was dressed in a holiday suit, with a large white collar and a shiny top hat, and he carried a stick and a small case. He was followed by a boy who staggered under the weight of a packing-case like the one which had just been placed on the roof of the coach.

'Guard, guard!' cried the Magician, 'kindly stow this case on the roof with great care. It contains red fire and magical apparatus, and if it gets knocked about I won't answer for the consequences.'

Touching his hat respectfully, the guard, assisted by the driver, pulled the Magician's case on to the roof and laid it carefully on top of the dogs' luggage. Toby held the reins, watching anxiously what was being done; while the Magician greeted Dennis with a cheerful smile and asked him whether he was going to the fair.

'Yes, Herr Magician, to the fair we are going undoubtedly,

18

perhaps,' Dennis replied.

'And where is your little friend Larry to-day?' the Magician asked.

'Busy!' shouted Toby nervously.

'Extremely busy,' Dennis added. 'So much has he to do that himself he has shut away where no one can perceive him. This very fortunate was, perhaps, because when the fares of Toby and I have been paid, only twopence will remain to enable us to amuse ourselves at Arkville. Unless some kind gentleman presents us with sixpence or so, was it?'

'Ah, yes; yes. Well, I hope you enjoy yourselves,' said the Magician hastily. And he climbed into the coach.

'Take your seats, everybody, please!' shouted the guard.

The coach-door was slammed, Dennis climbed up beside Toby, the driver cracked his whip, and the coach rattled under the gate and took the Arkville road. The guard blew a tootle on his little tin horn, and, encouraged by this, the horses broke into a gallop, while the passengers smiled happily at one another.

III

The coach rolled along for several miles and had just passed the cross-roads, when the travellers uttered a gasp of dismay. From a cluster of trees there cantered a black horse ridden by a rough-looking man wearing a long cloak and a black mask. He halted in the middle of the road and pointed at the driver a large pistol.

'Stand and deliver!' he cried.

'A highwayman!' said Toby. 'This is dreadful!'

'Never anything so dreadful have I seen, never!' remarked Dennis.

The coach pulled up with a jerk, and the highwayman rode forward. 'I want your valuables,' he said. 'So hurry up and

19

S·G·Hulme Beaman

hand them over!'

'No valuables we possess, Herr Highwayman,' said Dennis. 'Only our box upon the roof in which reposes one or two bones and a packet of dog-biscuits.'

'Ho, does it!' replied the highwayman. 'Then I shan't trouble to open that. What's in the other box?'

'Don't you touch my box!' shouted the Magician, stepping down. 'That contains most valuable magical apparatus, and if you open it I won't answer for the consequences.'

'Valuable, is it?' sneered the highwayman. 'Then I'll have a look inside that. Hand it down. Which is your box?'

'The underneath box,' replied the Magician.

'I think, Herr Magician——' began Dennis. And then he noticed that the Magician was frowning at him, and showing in the palm of his hand a bright half-crown. Dennis paused and thought hard; then he gave the Magician a sly wink.

'The Herr Magician is right,' he said. 'The underneath box

20

the valuable magic contains undoubtedly, perhaps.'

'Then fetch it down!' the highwayman ordered.

Looking rather frightened, the driver and the guard lifted the underneath box from the roof of the coach and laid it in the road.

'Now, stand back everyone,' said the highwayman. And, dismounting from his horse, he approached the box, pistol in hand.

The Magician looked most uneasy. He had hoped that the highwayman would have allowed them to drive away before he opened the box. When he saw the man preparing to examine it he knew that if bones and dog-biscuits were discovered inside, the highwayman would insist upon opening the other box as well.

'I really would advise you to leave that box alone, Mr. Highwayman,' he said in a quavering voice. 'It's very dangerous to meddle with magic.'

'I don't believe in magic,' replied the highwayman scornfully. And, with his free hand, he began to fumble at the cords.

Dennis took up a position behind the highwayman, and then spoke in a very loud voice.

'Most cautious be, Herr Highwayman. That box contains, very likely perhaps, a magical rabbit; a rabbit of the kind which the excellent Herr Magician from top-hats produces. That rabbit may out-spring with great violence. With very great violence it may out-spring upon you!'

'I'm not afraid of rabbits,' replied the highwayman. 'And I'm not deaf, so don't shout so!'

He untied the cord of the box and flung back the lid.

At once there was a cry of 'Baa!' and from the chest there shot, like a Jack-in-the-box, a woolly figure which struck the highwayman violently in the waistcoat.

With a startled cry the robber dropped his pistol and, at the same moment, Dennis and Toby leapt forward and fixed their

21

A struggling heap upon the roadway

jaws in his coat-tails. The driver and his companions also dashed forward; and in a moment there was a struggling heap upon the roadway, with the highwayman underneath.

When the robber had been overpowered, and tied up with the cord from the box, the Magician turned to the three animals with a smile.

'Excellent, excellent!' he said. 'We owe the capture of this desperate fellow to the presence of mind of these young animals.'

'Oh, yes, sir, you do,' replied Larry. 'But it was very difficult. When I heard the highwayman beginning to open the box I was awfully frightened, because I'm only a little lamb, and all lambs are timid. I could hardly keep from baaing. But then I heard Dennis shouting, and I knew what I had to do. So I tried to be brave, and did my little best.'

'You were brave,' the Magician told him. 'You undoubtedly saved us all.'

'Yes, but what I want to know is: what is all this?' asked the driver. 'How did you get inside that box? And whose box is it?'

'Oh, Mr. Driver, sir, we won't deceive you,' said Larry. 'Dennis and Toby and I wanted to go to the fair at Arkville, but we hadn't enough money. So we decided that I should go as luggage, because luggage is free. And I was shut up in the box, and you very kindly carried it to the coach.'

'Then it was a swindle!' cried the driver. 'You were trying to cheat the coach-company by travelling without paying your fare.'

'Oh, yes, Mr. Driver, sir, I see that now,' replied Larry. 'It was very wrong of us I know.'

'But remember, driver, that he saved us all from being robbed,' the Magician pointed out. 'And to save any trouble, and as a reward for this lamb's bravery, I will pay his fare.'

'Oh, thank you, Mr. Magician, sir,' said Larry.

Dennis sidled up to the Magician and remarked in a low

23

voice, 'Did I in your hand perceive a half-crown also, Herr Magician, when our box you claimed?'

'You did,' replied the Magician. 'And that half-crown I now have much pleasure in presenting to you.'

'Most grateful we are, Herr Magician,' said Dennis. 'Come, Larry and Toby my friends, let us again take our places upon this so-excellent coach and to the fair proceed. For there upon the roundabouts many rides we will enjoy.'

The Extraordinary Affair of Ernest the Policeman

ERNEST the policeman was walking home towards Toytown along the road from Arkville. It was night, and the constable was hurrying, for he had missed the last coach and was anxious to reach his little house by the police-station. His boots went plod, plod in the dusty road and he whistled a tune as he went, staring up at the stars and wondering how far away they were.

Ernest had passed the cross-roads when he suddenly stopped and listened. From a field on his right came a curious humming sound and a gentle thudding, and the policeman, leaning over a fence to look, perceived a little woolly figure which he had no difficulty in recognising as that of Larry the lamb. The little animal was dancing round in a circle on his back hoofs, swinging his front legs gracefully from side to side, and humming all the time in a hoarse, baahing voice.

'Hi, Larry, my lad!' Ernest called. 'What are you doing there?'

Larry immediately stopped dancing and, after staring nervously at Ernest for a few moments, ran towards him.

'Oh, Mr. Ernest, sir,' cried Larry. 'You did give me a start. I thought you were a fairy!'

'A fairy—me!' exclaimed Ernest. 'Do I look like a fairy?'

'Please, I don't know,' Larry said. 'I've never seen one.'

'Then be more careful what you say, Larry, my lad. What are you doing here at this time of night? Don't you know that all

'What are you doing here at this time of night?' said Ernest
lambs should be in bed?'

'Oh, Mr. Ernest, sir, I'm looking for toadstools,' said Larry.

'And don't you know you mustn't eat toadstools!' cried
Ernest. 'Has nobody never told you that toadstools will make
you ill?'

'But I don't want to eat them,' Larry exclaimed. 'You see,
my friend Dennis the dachshund lent me a book about fairies:
and the book said that at night fairies come out and dance
round toadstools. So I've been looking for toadstools, and
when I've found some I've been dancing round them. You see,
I thought that might make the fairies come out and dance too.'

Now Ernest did not believe in fairies: very few policemen do.
But he did not want to hurt Larry's feelings, so he just said:

'Ho, indeed. Well, Larry, my lad, I don't think you'd better
stay here any longer. I've never seen any fairies hereabouts: I
don't think they come so near the town as this.'

'Oh, but Mr. Ernest, sir; my friend Dennis has seen one!' cried Larry.

'Oh, he has, has he? Who says so?'

'He told me so himself,' replied Larry. 'And he ought to know.'

'He ought, certainly,' Ernest admitted. 'But if I was you I wouldn't believe everything that sausage-dog says, my lad. Not by no means I shouldn't. I notice he ain't out here looking for fairies himself; I reckon he's tucked up all snug and comfortable in his kennel.'

'Oh, no, he's not, Mr. Ernest, sir,' said Larry. 'He's over there in the field looking. He's digging holes to see if he can find any fairies. He's very clever at digging, Dennis is.'

'Digging, is he?' remarked Ernest. 'Then he's digging for rabbits, not fairies, I'll be bound. And if I catch him bringing home any rabbits I'll have the law on him. And while we're on the subject, my lad, do you see that notice-board? And if you do, can you read it?'

'Oh, yes, sir,' Larry replied. 'It says: "Trespassers will be prosecuted." I read that before we went into the field. I said to my friend Dennis: "Do you think we'd better trespass, because it must be dreadful to be prosecuted?" And he said: "Nonsense, they never prosecute lambs: lambs are supposed to run about in fields. It makes fields look more countryfied." So I trespassed and Dennis said he'd risk it, so we both trespassed.'

At that moment they heard a muffled barking.

'He's found one! said Larry. 'Dennis has found a fairy! Come on, Mr. Ernest, sir!'

'Not him,' said Ernest. 'He may have found something, but it's not a fairy.'

But he climbed the fence and followed Larry across the field in the direction of the barking. And very soon they came to a ring of toadstools near which was a large hole in the ground; and projecting from the hole were the tail and back legs of

27

Dennis the dachshund. He was wriggling and barking and appeared to be most excited.

'Here, you hound: what are you up to?' asked Ernest, prodding Dennis with his foot.

Dennis wriggled from the hole, and when he saw Ernest he looked rather nervous. But he quickly recovered and saluted the constably jauntily with his paw.

'What were you up to?' Ernest repeated.

'Up to anything I was not officer,' replied Dennis. 'I down a hole was.'

'Up or down, it don't make no difference,' said Ernest. 'What I want to know is: what were you a-doing of in that hole? What do you mean by going and digging up fields like that! Not only trespassing, but digging.'

'Well, officer, like this it was,' Dennis explained. 'I to my friend here said: 'For fairies let's go and look——'' '

'I know all about that,' Ernest interupted. 'I've heard about that from this young lamb. You've been a-putting silly ideas into the head of this innocent lamb. And not content with that you've been and gone and dug a hole. It's only because I'm not sure whether this field belongs to Toytown or Arkville that I don't take your name and address, my lad.'

'I a hole was not digging,' said Dennis. 'Of digging a hole I should not dream. Just making one larger I was doing. You see a fairy ran down this hole just now I'm sure I saw. At least, nearly sure. The moonlight deceived me I don't think.'

'No, nor you won't deceive me, my lad,' said Ernest.

'Oh, Dennis, what was it like?' cried Larry.

'To say it is difficult,' replied Dennis. 'You see rather dark it is. But to me like a very small person with butterfly wings it looked.'

'Ho, indeed!' said Ernest.

'Not half as big as the constable here,' Dennis continued, 'but much better-looking.'

28

'Ho, indeed!' said Ernest again.

'And it long white whiskers had,' Dennis added.

'Well, all I can say is I should like to see that there fairy,' remarked Ernest. 'Whiskers and all. And when I see it I'll believe it.'

'You've only got your face down that hole to put,' Dennis pointed out, 'and then you it would see, I no doubt have. To have gone far it cannot.'

'Only mind you don't get your face muddy, Mr. Ernest, sir,' Larry said.

'It's no part of a constable's duty to go a-shoving his head down holes,' said Ernest. 'Undignified, I call it. But just to show you two animals there ain't no fairy I will have a look.'

'Only do be careful not to get stuck, Mr. Ernest,' Larry cried.

'Yes, of that do be careful,' Dennis added. 'Dreadful it would be if so stuck you became. Without our Ernest what we should do I don't know.'

'Keep your remarks for them as wants them, my lad,' said Ernest sternly. 'You're being sarcastic, that's what you're being. I always knows when an animal is being sarcastic. You keep your remarks to yourself. Here, hold my helmet; and don't go trying it on. Either of you.'

Handing his helmet to Larry, Ernest went down on his hands and knees and peered into the hole. Then he put his arm down it, and after that the whole of his head. Presently he looked up, his face very red. 'It's quite a deep hole,' he said.

'Oh, Mr. Ernest, sir, there's a great, fat slug just going to crawl down your collar!' cried Larry. 'Keep quite still and I'll squash it with my little hoof.'

When the slug had been disposed of, Ernest again turned his attention to the hole. 'That's more than a hole, that is,' he remarked. 'That looks to me like a well or something. Or the way into a cave. This is beginning to look interesting, and I'd

29

Ernest the policeman disappeared from view

better see where it leads to.'

'Perhaps it leads to fairyland!' cried Larry.

'More likely to lead to the pond where the celluloid ducks live,' replied Ernest. 'Still, I'm a-going down it. I hope I know my duty, and it's clearly my duty to investigate this here hole.'

Without further words Ernest again knelt down and, after enlarging the hole with his hand, he thrust his head and shoulders into it and began to wriggle. After a few moments the earth round the edges suddenly gave way and Ernest the policeman disappeared from view. Larry and Dennis ran to the hole and looked down; but they could see nothing but darkness.

'He's gone,' said Larry.

'Quite,' Dennis agreed. 'And I hope he won't be long because I my tea want.'

'Tea? You mean supper,' said Larry.

'No, I don't, I my tea mean' replied Dennis. 'For tea this afternoon I was not at home; Mrs. Goose some tea gave me for watching some cakes she was baking. And, of course that as a proper tea I don't count. My tea and supper both together I will have when home we get; that time will save.'

'I hope Ernest won't be long,' remarked Larry. 'It's most awfully late. And I hope he won't get stolen by the fairies.'

'Of fairies stealing a policeman I have never heard,' Dennis

30

admitted, 'but of course, stranger things have happened. Why does not he hurry!'

But Ernest did not hurry up. In fact he did not come up at all. Larry and Dennis sat patiently on the grass waiting, and presently began to yawn. Then Larry's little head began to nod and Dennis began to snore. The both fell fast asleep.

★   ★   ★   ★   ★

Early the next morning the Mayor of Toytown was seated in his study at the Town Hall. He was feeling very annoyed and irritated, for he had been taken away from his breakfast before he had half finished and had only had time for one slice of marmalade. This was due to the fact that Mr. Growser had called, demanding to see the Mayor on most important business; and now the two gentlemen sat opposite each other while Mr. Growser was explaining why he had called.

'It's disgraceful!' Mr. Growser was saying. 'Disgraceful! It ought not ot be allowed. It wouldn't be allowed in any decent town. Where are the police? What are the police doing to allow such things to happen?'

'I don't know yet what has happened,' replied the Mayor. 'I must ask you to kindly explain, and not to shout so. Also kindly refrain from thumping your umbrella on my new carpet.'

'I shall thump my umbrella wherever I like and as hard as I like!' cried the old gentleman. 'It's only me that keeps this town awake. And now I have had one of my windows broken! Scandalous! Disgraceful!'

'Yes, but what has happened?' the Mayor asked.

'Don't I keep on telling you!' Mr. Growser cried. 'My window has been broken; my window! W-I-N-D-O—— window! Some one has thrown a stone through it!'

The Mayor rose from his chair and stared at Mr. Growser with great dignity. 'And did you tear me away from my breakfast just to tell me that one of your windows has been broken?'

he asked.

'No, sir, I did not!' replied Mr. Growser. 'I also desired to tell you that you ought to be ashamed to call yourself Mayor of a town where such things are allowed. I say what I think, sir. I say what I think. Breakfast indeed! You sit there gorging yourself with bread and treacle while the whole town is going to rack and ruin.'

'I'm afraid that the matter of broken windows is hardly my department, Mr. Growser,' said the Mayor. 'You should apply to the police. That is what the police are for.'

'Oh, indeed, Mr. Mayor! Indeed! I'm glad to know that; I have often wondered what the police were for. And now I do know I have no hesitation in saying that the police ought to be thoroughly ashamed of themselves!'

The Mayor was just about to utter a stern reply to this when his secretary came bustling in.

'Your worship,' said the secretary, 'two animals have arrived with some very curious news. It concerns the constable. You must have noticed he did not appear here this morning as usual; the animals in question seem to be in a rather excited state. They say they know why he is absent.'

'I know why he is absent!' cried Mr. Growser. 'He's ashamed to show his face. And no wonder!'

The Mayor ignored the old gentleman and ordered his secretary to admit the callers; and in a few moments Larry and Dennis stepped into the room. The lamb was carrying the policeman's helmet, and both animals looked very muddy and untidy.

'Oh, sir, oh, Mr. Mayor, sir!' began Larry.

'What is it, my lamb? What is it?' asked the Mayor. 'Take your time, my good animal, take your time.'

'Oh, sir, oh, sir, we've come to tell you about Mr. Ernest,' cried Larry.

'Ernest the constable that was,' Dennis added.

'This is a most extraordinary story,' said the Mayor

'That was! cried the Mayor. 'Isn't he still the constable?'

Dennis shook his head sadly and Larry rubbed his eyes with a very muddy little hoof.

'He's been stolen by the fairies,' said Larry.

'Stolen by what?' cried the Mayor.

'The fairies, Mr. Mayor, sir.'

'From under our very noses stolen,' Dennis added.

'Stuff and nonsense!' shouted Mr. Growser. 'Fairies indeed! Whoever heard of such a thing. He's afraid to face me, that's what it is. He's hiding. He's ashamed!'

'I feel sure you must be mistaken, my good animals,' remarked the Mayor. 'Quite apart from the fact that there is—ahem—some doubt as to whether there are—in short—such things as fairies, I certainly feel that it would take quite a lot of fairies to steal a large, able-bodied policeman. Did you actually witness the—ahem—kidnapping?'

'Well, you see, Mr. Mayor, sir, it was like this,' Larry explained. 'Me and my friend Dennis were out looking for fairies last night, and Mr. Ernest came along just when Dennis saw one. It ran down a deep hole. And Mr. Ernest said: 'I'd like

33

to see a fairy with long white whiskers.' And he looked. And then he said: 'Hold my helmet.' And we did, and he squeezed down the big hole and disappeared. So we waited and waited and he never came out again. And Dennis said: "By the fairies he has been stolen; we the Mayor must tell." And here we are. And this is Mr. Ernest's helmet he asked us to hold.'

'This is a most extraordinary story!' exclaimed the Mayor. 'Most extraordinary!'

'I don't believe a word of it,' said Mr. Growser. 'And for a policeman to be out looking for fairies when all the ruffians of Toytown are throwing stones at my windows is nothing short of a scandal. Yes, sir; a scandal. Have you two animals been throwing stones at my windows?'

'Oh, no, sir,' cried Larry. 'I never throw stones! Only mud-pies.'

'Then are you the animal who put a mud-pie in my letter-box six weeks ago come Wednesday?' asked Mr. Growser fiercly.

'I—I don't remember, sir,' Larry faltered.

'Tut, tut, Mr. Growser; never mind the mud-pies,' said the Mayor. 'Let us consider this matter of our very romantic policeman. The theory advanced by these young animals is ingenious, but I think it more likely that the unlucky constable has simply fallen into a deep hole.'

'Then I hope he is being nibbled by rabbits at this very moment!' cried Mr. Growser. 'It would serve him right. Gallivanting after fairies while my windows are being broken. Disgraceful!'

'I feel it is my duty as Mayor of Toytown to try and rescue the constable, fairies or no fairies,' the Mayor announced. 'I shall proceed to the hole immediately.'

'And I will come with you,' said Mr. Growser. 'I intend to tell this policeman what I think of his conduct.'

'Then we will make up a search-party,' the Mayor continued. 'I think we had better have the Inventor with us; he is such a clever fellow that if the officer is stuck or anything like that, he may be able to suggest a convenient way of getting him out. The Magician might also be useful in case there are any fairies to be dealt with; he could do a spell or something.'

So the Mayor sent his secretary with notes to the Inventor and the Magician, and presently those two gentlemen arrived, the Inventor carrying several appliances which he thought might come in useful, and the Magician with an attache case containing a selection of spells. Then the whole party set off for the hole in the field.

★   ★   ★   ★   ★

When they arrived at the field in which the mysterious disappearance of Ernest had taken place, Larry and Dennis experienced some difficulty, at first, in finding the hole; there were so many holes. But at last they decided upon one particular hole, very much larger than any other, as that down which Ernest had wriggled. The entire party gathered round this and examined carefully. Then the Mayor knelt down and called: 'Officer! Officer, are you there? He doesn't seem to be coming out,' he added, looking up.

'He's ashamed to come out, that's what it is,' said Mr. Growser. 'Ashamed; and I'm not surprised.'

'Well, what had we better do?' the Mayor inquired. 'Can any one offer a suggestion? What is the best thing to do when a policeman has fallen into a hole?'

'Let him stop there,' replied Mr. Growser in a decided voice. 'Let him stop there and get another policeman.'

'Well, of course, Mr. Mayor,' the Magician remarked, 'if he has been stolen by fairies I think the best thing to do is for me to draw a magic circle round the hole and to make one of my well-known spells. I only use the best materials for my spells, so I feel sure that should work.'

'I cannot agree, Mr. Magician,' said the Inventor. 'The matter seems to me perfectly simple; perfectly simple. All we have to do is to place a packet of my special gunpowder in the hole, light a long fuse and then all return to the other side of the field. Then when the gunpowder explodes it ought to blow the constable out of the hole.'

'Oh, sir,' cried Larry, 'it might blow him farther in!'

'True, it might,' the Inventor agreed. 'But then again it might not. It might, for example, blow him out of one of the other holes.'

'That's a splendid idea!' said the Mayor. 'A splendid idea! The only thing is it might blow him out in pieces, which would be most awkward and inconvenient.'

'Yes, I never thought of that,' remarked the Inventor. 'Well, here is another idea. I have a nice piece of rope here and a lot of fishing-hooks. We might tie a bundle of fish-hooks to the end of the rope, lower it into the hole and fish for him. If we find the hooks catch in anything we can all pull together. That ought to fetch him out.'

Everyone agreed that this was an excellent idea; so the hooks were fastened to the rope and each of the party took it in turns to fish for Ernest. But although they brought up a toffee tin and an old boot—which did not seem to belong to the constable—they were not successful in rescuing Ernest.

'Now perhaps you'll allow me to try,' said the Magician. 'You've messed about with ropes and fish-hooks and things, and we're no nearer. We will now see what can be done with a little high-class magic. Could any one oblige me with a match?'

The Magician drew a large circle round the hole, lit some red fire in a tin and then read several spells out of a little book which he drew from his pocket. The red fire smelled rather nasty and made everyone cough, but just as it burned down and the Magician finished reading, the Mayor uttered a shout and pointed. Out from the hole crawled a very fat white rabbit.

'There,' said the Magician, closing his book with a snap. 'It was perfectly simple, you see. There he is.'

36

The party returned to Toytown

'But that's not the policeman, that's a rabbit!' cried the Mayor.

'You'll pardon me, Mr. Mayor; that is the policeman. He's simply been turned into a rabbit by the fairies.' the Magician told him. 'I knew that had probably happened; of course, it was obvious to a person like myself skilled in every form of magic. Let me give you my card in case you should want any little spell done at any time.'

'Rubbish! Stuff and nonsense!' Mr. Growser shouted, 'its absurd. I don't believe in fairies; I don't believe in anything. I don't even believe in Father Christmas.'

'Shame!' cried Dennis. 'Larry, my friend, in Father Christmas he doesn't believe.'

'Oh, sir,' said Larry, 'you'll never get anything in your sock next Christmas if you talk like that!'

In the meantime the Mayor had succeeded in catching the white rabbit and was making chirruping noises at it. 'It is Ernest, I feel sure,' he said. 'He seems to know me.'

'Oh, yes, Mr. Mayor, sir,' cried Larry. 'It's Mr. Ernest. You can tell by his goggly eyes. His eyes always looked poppy like that.'

'Well, all we can do is to take him home and treat him kindly,' said the Mayor. 'Perhaps in time it will wear off.'

'Certainly, certainly,' agreed the Magician. 'I should say that in a month or so, if you treat the officer kindly and give him plenty of fresh bran, he will be himself again.'

So, carrying the rabbit very carefully, the party returned to Toytown.

★   ★   ★   ★   ★

On the following day the Mayor stood looking at the white rabbit. It lay on a bed of hay in a nice roomy cage which the Inventor had very kindly sat up all night to make; but although it was a very fine cage for a rabbit it was hardly large enough for a policeman. The Mayor was wondering whether the rabbit would turn back into Ernest quite suddenly—in which case he was likely to get uncomfortably squashed—or whether the change would take place gradually, in which case they might be able to pull Ernest through the door of the cage before he got too large.

Beside the Mayor stood Larry the lamb holding a large bunch of groundsel, portions of which he was offering to the rabbit.

'He doesn't seem to like it very much, Mr. Mayor,' said Larry. 'And I got up early to pick it for him. Because I thought "Mr. Ernest was so nice and kind to me when he was a policeman, so I must be kind to him now he's a rabbit." '

'Very nice of you, my lamb. Very nice of you,' replied the Mayor.

'You see, when Mr. Ernest changes back again to a policeman we want him to say:' "Every one was kind to me when I was a rabbit. They gave me fresh hay every morning, and plenty of nice groundsel; so it wasn't so bad being a rabbit." It's very disappointing that he doesn't seem to like groundsel. Perhaps I'd better go out and pick him some chickweed.'

As the Mayor had never kept rabbits he was not quite sure

what kind of food was most suitable; and they were still discussing the matter when they heard footsteps in the corridor outside, the loud thumping of an umbrella on the floor, and into the room there stumped Mr. Growser followed by Mrs. Goose, the lady who kept the confectioner's shop.

'There you are, madam, there you are,' said Mr. Growser. 'There is the Mayor. Tell your story to him: he has nothing to do but play with rabbits. No doubt he can find time to listen.'

'Whatever is all this?' asked the Mayor. 'Good-morning, Mrs. Goose; pardon me for receiving you without my gold chain, but I've only just finished breakfast. What can I have the pleasure of doing for you this morning?'

'Oh, your worship, whatever shall I do?' cried Mrs. Goose. 'Whatever shall I do? I have been looking for the policeman.'

'The policeman?' said the Mayor. 'Well, as a matter of fact, I'm afraid the policeman is not quite himself at the moment, Mrs. Goose. He is hardly in a position to attend to his duties.'

'That's what I told this good lady,' Mr. Growser interrupted. 'I told her the officer was playing at being a rabbit, and I also told her what I thought of his conduct. I will repeat my remarks if you wish.'

'No, no, Mr. Growser,' the Mayor cried hastily. 'There is no need: I am sure we all understand.'

'Oh, your worship,' said Mrs. Goose, 'I have been running round the streets looking for the policeman, and I met this gentleman who kindly brought me to see you. I'm in terrible trouble. There is a great, big robber in my cellar!'

'A robber in your cellar!' cried the Mayor.

'Yes, your worship. The cellar where I keep my stock of sweets, and cakes, and all the sugar and currants and things I make them with. I went in early this morning with a candle, and there was a great dirty-looking man sitting in the corner eating my cakes. I was so frightened I dropped the candle and ran out. I locked the cellar door, so he's still there. Whatever

39

shall I do?'

'This is a serious matter,' said the Mayor. 'I will see into it at once. As the policeman is not available I, personally, will proceed to your cellar, màdam, and arrest this robber.'

'Oh, your worship, you are brave!' cried Mrs. Goose.

'Not at all, madam, not at all,' said the Mayor. 'I will take a thick stick with me, in case the fellow turns violent, and perhaps Mr. Growser will come with me and lend me his support.'

'I certainly will!' exclaimed Mr. Growser. 'I shall be glad of the opportunity of telling the robber what I think of him. He ought to be ashamed, eating the poor woman's cakes!'

So they all, including Larry the lamb, set out for Mrs. Goose's shop, and on the way they met Dennis the dachshund who also joined the party. The Mayor led the way down to the cellar, holding a lighted candle in one hand and his stick in the other; Mr. Growser unlocked the door and they both rushed into the cellar.

'Come out, you scoundrel!' cried the Mayor. 'Surrender!'

'You ought to be ashamed of yourself!' shouted the old gentleman.

A large and very untidy figure arose from the corner of the cellar and blinked in the light of the candle. He was covered with mud, grass was sticking out of his hair, and his mouth was smeared with jam.

'Good-morning, your worship,' said the figure.

'Why, it's Ernest the policeman!' cried the Mayor.

'And he's broken into my cellar to steal my cakes!' cried Mrs. Goose, who had followed down the stairs.

'Oh, Mr. Ernest, sir, how greedy of you!' said Larry. 'And after me giving you all that groundsel!'

'Oh, but——' the Mayor stammered. 'Why, there must be a mistake somewhere. If this is the policeman he certainly can't be that rabbit. The Magician misinformed us regarding that

40

The little animal was dancing round in a circle *(page 25)*

'Do you see that notice board? and if you do, can you read it?' *(page 27)*

'Here, you hound: What are you up to?' asked Ernest (*page 28*)

He thrust his head and shoulders into the hole and began to wriggle (*page 30*)

'Well, what had we better do?' the Mayor inquired (*page 35*)

The red fire smelled rather nasty and made everyone cough (*page 36*)

Out from the hole crawled a very fat white rabbit (*page 36*)

rabbit.'

'Rabbit, rabbit!' cried Ernest. 'What rabbit?'

'We'll tell you all about that another time,' said the Mayor hastily. 'In the meantime will you kindly explain, officer, what you are doing in Mrs. Goose's cellar?'

'Oh, it's Mrs. Goose's cellar, is it?' replied Ernest.

'You ought to know, officer, you ought to know,' Mr. Growser shouted. 'You've got her strawberry jam all over your face! You ought to be ashamed; your duty is to arrest robbers, not to set them an example like this!'

'It ain't strawberry jam, it's raspberry,' said Ernest. 'If you listen I'll explain.'

'I proceeded to crawl along the tunnel,' Ernest continued. 'It was a very tight fit, and I nearly got stuck several times. But after crawling for miles and miles——'

'For how far?' cried the Mayor.

'For a considerable distance—my head suddenly came out into an open space, for, your worship, I was crawling head first as you might say. I pulled myself after my head and fell out on to the floor of this here place.'

'This, thought I, is an underground cave or such like; and I proceeded to investigate. It was very dark and I couldn't see nothing, but I found it was full of stuff to eat. And then I couldn't find the entrance to the tunnel again so I had to stop where I was. And to prevent myself from starving, as you might say, I had to eat some of the stuff I found here. And that's all, and very pleased I am to see your worship.'

'A most extraordinary affair!' cried the Mayor.

'Most suspicious,' said Mr. Growser. 'I regard the whole story with the gravest suspicion.'

'I can see one thing,' said Mrs. Goose. 'Some one has been digging a secret tunnel to my cellar in order to steal my cakes and things.'

'Not a doubt of it, ma'am,' replied Ernest. 'And your cellar is

41

only just inside the wall of the town, so it wasn't so very difficult to do. But what I want to know is, who done it?'

'Yes, who done—that is to say, did it!' cried the Mayor. 'It must have been some one very skilled in digging.'

'Who could it have been!' cried Larry. 'It is curious, isn't it, Dennis?'

But there was no reply from Dennis, who had silently crept up the stairs and disappeared.

'I have my suspicions,' said Ernest. 'I don't know nothing, of course, but I always was rather good at guessing. So if you will now excuse me, ladies and gentlemen, I will now resume my duties. I shall first have a nice wash and make myself tidy as befits an officer of the law. Then I am going to have a good breakfast, and after that——'

'Oh, what will you do after that, Mr. Ernest, sir?' asked Larry.

'After that,' said Ernest, 'I am going to have a little conversation with your friend Dennis the dachshund.'

A Portrait of the Mayor

DOWN by the river, in a part of Toytown which is considered not very respectable, stands Mr. Brass's shop; and over the shop is a room which, at the time this story opens, lived an artist. He was not often seen because he was of a shy and retiring disposition, and when he did appear in the streets the more common animals shouted rude remarks, and even went so far as to throw mud at him. To some extent this was due to his artistic dress, which consisted of a black velvet coat, orange tie, green and white check trousers and white spats. However, the behaviour of the animals was such that, instead of walking about the streets during the day, the artist preferred to stay at home and paint pictures, emerging cautiously at night after the animals had gone to bed.

One evening Mr. Growser, who lived in Ark Street, heard a timid knock at the door and when, grumbling and complaining, he opened it there upon the doorstep stood the Artist. He held a large, flat parcel under his arm and from this he drew a sheet of cardboard and held it under Mr. Growser's nose.

'Would you like to buy a picture?' he asked. 'Very nice; very cheap.'

'Buy a what!' cried Mr. Growser. 'Do you mean to say you have knocked at my door to sell me something! It ought not to be allowed! Disturbing respectable citizens at this time of night!'

43

'Well, buy a picture and I'll go away. Very nice; very cheap.'

'A picture? A picture? Let me look at what you have the impudence to call a picture,' said Mr. Growser, adjusting his spectacles and staring very hard. 'Ah! What is it?'

'A picture,' replied the Artist. 'Very nice——'

'Yes, yes I know. But what is it a picture of?'

'This is a shipwreck,' said the Artist.

'A shipwreck! A shipwreck!' Mr. Growser cried. 'But it's not a bit like a shipwreck. I wonder you are not ashamed of yourself! What's all that smoke, and all those twiddley things?'

'Oh, I beg your pardon,' said the Artist. 'I was showing you the wrong one. That's a railway-accident; but it's a very nice picture. This is the shipwreck.' And he showed Mr. Growser another picture.

'Ah, indeed,' observed the old gentleman. 'Well, I don't see very much difference between them. And in any case if I bought a picture I should want something more cheerful than those. I shouldn't dream of buying a picture in any case——'

'Very nice; very cheap,' the Artist muttered.

'——but if I did it would have to be something amusing.'

'Well, how about this one?' said the Artist. 'This is a picture of a baby elephant lost in the snow. You can see the tears running down his trunk and freezing.'

'But it's absurd; I never heard of such a thing! You have the impudence to show me a picture of an elephant lost in the snow, but where elephants live there isn't any snow. An elephant couldn't get lost in snow! I wonder you can look me in the face!'

'Perhaps the elephant was brought there by a circus,' the Artist suggested.

'Then in that case you ought to show the circus disappearing in the distance; else how are people to know? You come here knocking at doors and annoying people——'

'I've got a lot more,' the Artist said. 'Here is the Theatre Royal being blown up with gunpowder; and this is the police-

44

'This is a picture of a baby elephant,' said the Artist

station after a disastrous fire.'

'Go away! Go away!' cried Mr. Growser. 'I don't want to buy your pictures; I don't like your pictures. I don't like you either. And I don't like to be knocked up at this time of night; it ought not to be allowed.'

And he slammed the door.

The Artist turned away and, passing round the corner (for Mr. Growser's was a corner house) knocked at the first door he came to. And Mr. Growser opened that door.

'Like to buy a picture?' said the Artist. 'Very nice; very cheap.'

'How dare you!' cried the old gentleman. 'First you knock at my front door and then you knock at my side door. You ought to be ashamed of yourself. Go away! Go away!'

'Are you sure you wouldn't like to buy a picture?' the Artist inquired. 'I have a lot here, and a lot more at home.'

45

'I am absolutely positive on the subject. I was never more certain of anything in my life!' cried Mr. Growser.

'Well, would you like me to paint your front door, or your gate?' asked the Artist. 'I'd do it very nicely and very cheaply.'

Mr. Growser was too angry to reply. He slammed the door so violently that the Artist jumped and dropped his parcel of pictures; and, just as he picked it up and turned to go, he saw coming round the corner two figures of Larry the lamb and Dennis the dachshund. They were walking arm in arm and singing; Dennis in a very deep, guttural voice, and Larry in a little bleating treble.

'Oh, Dennis!' cried Larry. 'What a funny-looking man!'

'So! It is the Artist,' said Dennis. 'Over the shop of Mr. Brass he lives. All the low dogs of the street know him; frequently mud at him they throw and rude cries shout.'

'What are you staring at me like that for?' the Artist asked.

'Oh, sir, oh, sir, you do look so funny!' said Larry. 'But we don't wish to be rude, so we won't look at you if you don't like it.'

'I suppose you wouldn't like to buy a picture, either of you?' said the Artist.

'Oh, no, sir,' cried Larry. 'You see we haven't any money; I've spent all my pocket-money. We've been to a party at the Ark, and as it was the baby hippo's birthday I had to take him some lollipops.'

'A lovely party it was,' Dennis added.

'What did you have to eat?' the Artist inquired.

'Well, first of all, after we'd finished the lollipops I gave the baby hippo, we had some cream buns——'

'Cream buns!' cried the Artist.

'Yes, I love cream buns, and so does Dennis; only I always think they're very difficult to eat because when you bite them, if you're not very careful, they squirt.'

'And after that,' said Dennis, 'some jelly we had; also some lovely liver sausage. Two helpings of that I had.'

'But I am not very fond of sausage,' Larry went on, 'so I had two extra large helpings of birthday cake instead.'

'And after that——' began Dennis.

'Don't tell me any more!' cried the Artist.

'Oh, sir, we won't if it makes you jealous,' said Larry. 'Oh, please will you let us look at your pictures? I love looking at pictures. I used to know an artist who painted pictures once; he sat outside the fish-shop at Arkville, but his pictures were not painted on paper like yours; they were done on wooden boards which made them much stronger. People used to put pennies in his hat for looking at them.'

'What is that you say, my friend?' Dennis asked.

'People used to put pennies in the Artist's hat,' said Larry. 'He got quite a lot of pennies. I wish I could paint pictures; then I could get pennies too.'

'Ha! My friends, an idea I have!' cried Dennis. 'A splendid idea. An idea that will make us all rich. Many more pictures you have got, perhaps, was it, Mr. Artist?'

'Hundreds,' replied the Artist. 'Hundreds and hundreds. I could plaster the streets of Toytown with my pictures; but if I did Ernest the policeman would probably take my name and address.'

'Yes, he's very particular,' Larry agreed.

'Listen, my friends,' said Dennis. 'Let us all to the barn proceed, over a little refreshment there my great idea to discuss.'

'Refreshment! What sort of refreshment?' asked the Artist.

Dennis removed the peaked cap which he wore and from it produced two buns, a large bar of chocolate and half a sausage.

'See!' he cried. 'This food was from the party I saved. I was thrifty, was I not? Ha, ha!'

'Oh, Dennis, how greedy!' said Larry. 'And after eating all you did at the party!'

47

'In my kennel there was also a bone,' Dennis continued. 'But perhaps our Artist friend does not a bone appreciate?'

'I should certainly prefer the sausage,' the Artist admitted.

'Come then, my friends,' said Dennis. 'Let us to the barn proceed where quietly we may discuss this great idea which to me has come.'

'Oh yes, let's,' cried Larry.

'By all means,' the Artist agreed. 'Would you like me to carry the refreshments?'

★ ★ ★ ★ ★

Some days later Ernest the policeman left his house by the police-station immediately after breakfast, and proceeded towards the Town Hall in order to report to the Mayor before going on duty. But as he turned from Ark Street into the Square he paused and rubbed his eyes, for he was confronted by a most unusual sight. About a dozen pictures were propped against a wall or lay upon the pavement, and in the midst of them sat the small figure of Larry the lamb holding between his hoofs an old top hat. Ernest the policeman crossed the road and, standing in front of Larry, stared first at the pictures and then at the lamb.

'What's all this?' asked Ernest

'Oh, Mr. Ernest, sir, will you spare a penny?' Larry bleated.

'A penny!' cried Ernest. 'What for?'

'For a poor artist,' replied Larry. 'I've spent all my pocket-money this week, so I'm doing this to get some more. You can put the penny in my hat, Mr. Ernest, sir, and will you please make it two half-pennies instead of one penny, and then I can start rattling?'

'I'm none too sure that this sort of thing ain't against the law, my lad,' said Ernest. 'Pictures are all very well in their place; I like a nice almanac as much as anybody, but sticking them about the streets like this may give the town a bad name. I didn't know before that you could paint pictures.'

48

They approached Larry and looked at the pictures in silence

'Oh, Mr. Ernest, sir, didn't you?' said Larry.

'No, I didn't, my lad. And when I look at what you've done I ain't any too sure of it now. However, it is my duty to speak to his worship the Mayor before permitting this here show to continue. No doubt you'll hear from me again, my lad.'

Ernest walked away in a dignified manner, crossed the Square and entered the Town Hall. Larry waited nervously and presently the constable reappeared followed by the Mayor. They approached Larry and stood looking at the pictures in silence for some minutes.

'Oh, sir, oh, Mr. Mayor, sir,' Larry bleated. 'Please spare a penny for a poor artist!'

'That's what he said to me, sir,' remarked Ernest. 'Asked for two half-pennies, he did, so that he could rattle them.'

'Ha, indeed!' said the Mayor. 'Well, this appears to be a most talented lamb. I had no idea he could paint pictures. They strike me as being very good pictures—for a lamb. I doubt if you could do as well, officer.'

'Ah, then you haven't seen my notice-board outside the police-station with the portraits of highwaymen and all?'

'Quite, quite. However, I consider these to be most promising. Most promising. Tell me, my lamb, what does this picture represent?'

'Oh, sir, that's a little baby elephant lost in the snow,' Larry replied. 'If you look carefully you will see tears rolling down his little trunk and freezing.'

'Ah, yes; I can perceive them quite distinctly. A most affecting picture. Most affecting. And what is this one?

'Oh, please, Mr. Mayor, sir, that's the police-station after a disastrous fire,' Larry told him.

'I consider that to be a most disrespectful picture, your worship,' Ernest observed. 'Making fun of the police, that's what that is.'

'Oh, come, officer; don't be so touchy!' said the Mayor. 'I see nothing wrong with the picture, and I feel sure no one will recognise the police-station.'

'There's something in that, sir,' Ernest admitted. 'But it's disrespectful, all the same.'

'On the whole I consider this lamb should be encouraged,' said the Mayor. 'He is clearly a most talented animal. Here are two halfpennies for you, my lamb. Now tell me? do you think you could paint my portrait?'

'O, sir, oh, sir——' began Larry.

'I have long thought that the Town Hall should contain a portrait of its mayor; this seems an admirable opportunity for procuring one. Don't you think so, officer?'

'I don't see no harm in it, your worship. So long as you keep it inside the Town Hall,' Ernest replied.

'Very well, then. Now, my lamb, you are so talented that I feel sure you will be able to produce an excellent portrait of your Mayor. Bring your chalks, or your paints, or whatever you use, to the Town Hall to-morrow afternoon, when I shall be pleased to stand in a dignified attitude for you to paint me. Here is two and sixpence on account. Good-morning, my lamb; good-morning.'

'Oh, sir, oh, Mr. Mayor, sir——' Larry bleated after him. But the Mayor and Ernest had hurried away. Larry, looking most nervous and frightened, rapidly packed up his pictures and, placing the top-hat on his head, ran as hard as he could towards Mr. Brass's shop.

★   ★   ★   ★   ★

In the room above the shop of Mr. Brass, the Artist and Dennis the dachshund were engaged in counting a pile of coppers when Larry the lamb dashed in; and he looked so rumpled and frightened, while his hat had fallen so far over his little nose that his friends stared at him in astonishment.

'Oh, Dennis, oh, Mr. Artist, sir!' cried Larry. 'What do you think has happened? The Mayor gave me half a crown——'

'Half a crown!' said Dennis. 'Splendid. That was another tenpence for each of us was. With what we here have we well have done; well we have done. And all through my splendid idea.'

'It certainly was a good idea,' the Artist admitted.

'It was; rich we shall become,' said Dennis. 'It is well you met me, my friend. For business no head you have. Now what we must do is this: I have this morning in Noah Street one and sixpence collected; our friend here has half a crown obtained. Let us, so encouraged, our operations extend. Let us Toby the dog hire and all the other animals we can find, each with a pile of your pictures to sit. Each shall a separate street take, and each one half his takings to us shall pay. Splendid, was it not?'

'It sounds too good to be true,' said the Artist. 'There's a catch in it, somewhere.'

'Oh, yes, there is, there is!' cried Larry. 'I've found the catch. The Mayor is the catch. I've got to go to the Town hall to-morrow and paint his portrait. And I can't paint, because

51

you see I am only a little lamb.'

'Ha, this was awkward; very awkward, was it not?' observed Dennis.

'Very awkward indeed,' the Artist agreed. 'Because when the Mayor finds out that this lamb can't paint pictures he'll know the whole thing is a swindle.'

'A swindle! swindle! Talk not so, my friend!' cried Dennis. 'This was not a swindle; business it was. Let us think, let us think, Ha, I have it! You, Mr. Artist, a picture of the Mayor must paint. With it our friend to the Town Hall shall go. Then, after pretending the Mayor to paint, he will the picture show. Clever, was it not? Ha, ha!'

'Yes, it's a very good idea,' the Artist agreed. 'The only trouble is I've never seen the Mayor. I don't know what he looks like.'

'Never seen the Mayor!' cried Larry. 'Oh, Mr. Artist, sir, where were you brought up?'

'So; our friend has never the Mayor seen,' said Dennis. 'But what matters it? He must guess what the Mayor looks like; surely it was not difficult. Is he not an artist?'

'Well, of course, I know what he ought to look like,' said the Artist. 'Every one knows what a mayor ought to look like. I'll do my best; I'll start work at once. I suppose neither of you fellows have such a thing as a nice cream bun about you? There's nothing like a nice cream bun when one has an important piece of work to do.'

'Oh, sir, we haven't!' cried Larry. 'But if you promise to start work at once I'll go round to Mrs. Goose's and buy one.'

'And I, my friends, out into the streets will go to find animals who in this great idea of mine will join,' said Dennis.

Then the Artist set to work and painted hard, while Larry either watched him or ran backwards and forwards to Mrs. Goose's for further supplies of buns. And at last the picture was finished.

Larry looked at it doubtfully. 'It's not very like the Mayor,'

The Mayor struck an attitude of great dignity

he said. 'I don't believe he'll think it's a very good portrait.'

'Not like the Mayor!' cried the Artist. 'But I'm sure you couldn't have a better portrait of a mayor than that.'

'Oh, very well, sir, if you say so,' said Larry. 'You know best. I'll take it with me and pretend. And if he says it is not very good I shall just tell him it's the best I can do. After all, he ought not to expect anything much better from a lamb!'

★   ★   ★   ★   ★

At the appointed time Larry presented himself at the Town Hall. He carried a large parcel under his arm, an easel on his back, and he wore a large, orange-coloured tie, which the Artist had assured him was the correct thing to wear. He felt very nervous, and when the Mayor's secretary admitted him, Larry, for some moments, could only utter little feeble 'baah's.'

'Oh, sir, oh, sir,' he said at last. 'I've come to paint the portrait of the Mayor! He said I was to. I've got my box of paints here, and this is my easel.'

The secretary led the lamb to the Mayor's study where the

53

Mayor was walking up and down, wearing a new blue coat and his gold chain. 'Ah, my lamb; there you are then,' he said. 'What have you got on your back; a Punch and Judy show?'

'Oh, no, sir, that's my easel,' Larry explained. And I've got my box of paints, too, and a lot of paper.'

'Then we'll start at once. Now tell me: where would you like to sit?'

'Oh, sir, I'll sit over here in this corner,' replied Larry.

'But it's quite dark there!' the Mayor pointed out.

'It doesn't matter, Mr. Mayor, sir,' said Larry. 'I can paint just as well in the dark as I can in the light.'

'Very well; you know your own business best. Now I have decided to stand for my portrait in a very dignified way, holding a roll of paper; and you might put a picture of the Town Hall in the background. How would that do?'

'Oh, yes, just as you please, Mr. Mayor, sir; it's all the same to me. Would you like to see my little tubes of paint before I start? I unscrew the tops with my little teeth and squash the tubes with my hoofs and lovely little worms of colour come out. I love doing it.'

'I have no wish to see the coloured worms, my lamb,' replied the Mayor. 'And kindly refrain from squashing them on my new carpet. Also be careful not to splash the walls as you paint.'

Whereupon the Mayor struck an attitude of great dignity, one hand on his hip and the other grasping a long roll of paper, while Larry, concealed behind his easel in the dark corner, pretended to work very hard. But really he was amusing himself by squeezing all the little paint-tubes in the box which the Artist had lent him, and watching the coloured worms spread out over a sheet of cardboard. But after a very long time, when Larry had squeezed all the paint-tubes flat, and the Mayor had begun to sigh and pant in his efforts to retain the dignified attitude which he had chosen, the latter suddenly said.

'Have you nearly finished, my lamb? Because I am beginning to feel a trifle exhausted.'

'Oh, yes, Mr. Mayor, sir; I've quite finished if you have', replied Larry.

'Very well then,' said the Mayor. 'Now let me see what you have made of me.'

Very nervously Larry emerged from behind his easel with a picture on a piece of cardboard which he held beneath the Mayor's nose. The Mayor looked at it for some moments in silence.

'But—ahem—it doesn't look very much like me,' he said. 'In fact, I may say that it isn't a bit like me.'

'Oh, Mr. Mayor, sir, don't say that!' cried Larry.

'Why, I'm not as thin as that! I don't think any one would call me fat, but I am not thin. And I was holding a roll of paper, but in this picture I'm holding an umbrella!'

Larry peered at the picture. 'Oh, sir, it does look something like an umbrella, doesn't it?'

'And you have given me long white whiskers!' cried the Mayor.

'Oh, Mr. Mayor, sir, I don't think those are really meant for whiskers,' replied Larry. 'I think they are smudges.'

'And worse than all,' cried the Mayor, 'instead of putting the Town Hall in the background, you've painted in a tumble-down building which looks like the Dog and Whistle. Really, my lamb, I can hardly call this a good portrait; in fact, it isn't a portrait at all. It's just a rather messy picture of an unpleasant-looking old man with white whiskers leaning on an umbrella outside the Dog and Whistle.'

'Oh, sir, oh, Mr. Mayor, sir, I did my little best,' Larry bleated.

Before the Mayor could reply, there came a clatter of foot-steps, and into the room dashed Mr. Growser, closely followed by Ernest the policeman.

'This is disgraceful; disgraceful!' cried Mr. Growser. 'What

55

is the town coming to? Answer me that, sir; answer me that! Are you, or are you not, the Mayor of Toytown? And if the reply is in the affirmative, what do you mean by it?'

'Mean by what?' asked the Mayor testily. 'Kindly refrain from shouting in that rude manner. Mr. Growser.'

'The whole town is simply infested with artists!' cried Mr. Growser. 'You can't take a step without tripping over them; not a step. They are like black-beetles. It's disgraceful! It ought not to be allowed!'

'The fact of the matter is, your worship,' Ernest explained, 'that in every street in the town there seems to be an animal sitting on the pavements with a lot of pictures round him and a cap in front of him, a-shouting and a-howling for pennies. Awful it is, sir; you never see such a thing.'

'Like—like—cockroaches!' shouted Mr. Growser.

'This is extremely curious,' said the Mayor. 'I thought this lamb was the only artist we had in the town.'

'Then you thought wrongly, sir,' cried Mr. Growser. 'For one of them knocked at my door the other night and had the impudence to ask if I would buy one of his pictures. A horrible looking man with an orange tie—like that lamb there—and white spats. Yes, sir; white spats! Disgraceful; they ought not to be allowed!'

'And he asked you to buy one of his pictures?' said the Mayor curiously.

'He called them pictures!' One of them pretended to show a young elephant lost in the snow; a ridiculous thing. And another was supposed to represent the police-station after a fire. They were horrible; horrible. I told him so; I never mince my words, sir; never.'

'Oh, Mr. Mayor, sir, if you'll excuse me, I think I'll go now,' Larry bleated.

'One moment, my lamb, one moment,' said the Mayor. 'There is something very curious here. These pictures which

56

'Would you like to buy a picture?' the Artist asked *(page 43)*

Ernest the Policeman stared first at the pictures and then at the Lamb (*page 48*)

Larry and Dennis with the Artist in his studio (*page 51*)

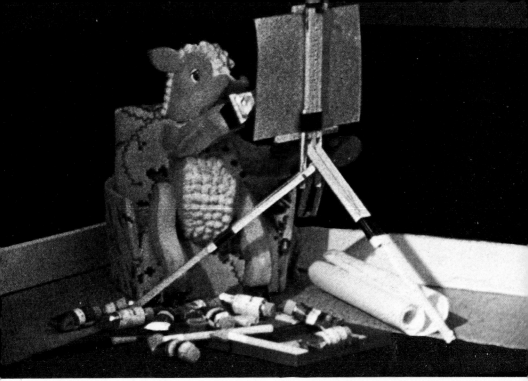

'Oh, sir, I'll sit over here in this corner,' replied Larry (*page 54*)

'Oh, sir, oh, Mr Mayor, sir, I did my little best,' Larry bleated
(*page 55*)

'Oh, Mr Mayor, sir, if you'll excuse me, I think I'll go now,' Larry bleated (*page 56*)

Mr. Growser mentions seem to be very like two you showed me. Now, my lamb, let us have the truth. Did you, or did you not, paint those pictures?'

'Oh, sir, oh, Mr. Mayor, sir, I won't deceive you,' cried Larry. 'I didn't. I can't paint pictures at all; you see my little hoofs are so awkward for holding brushes and things.'

'But how about this so-called portrait?' asked the Mayor, holding it up.

'Oh, sir, I didn't do that either; I only pretended. You see all the pictures were painted by an artist-gentleman who lives over Mr. Brass's shop. He's got hundreds and hundreds of pictures. And my friend Dennis thought it would be a splendid idea if we sat on the pavement with some pictures, because the people would give us pennies. And now Dennis has got all his friends to sit about with the pictures, and they have to give half the pennies they collect to Dennis and the artist-gentleman, because Dennis thought of it.'

'But this portrait?' cried the Mayor.

'Oh, sir, the artist-gentleman painted that for me to bring here. But my little conscience has been troubling me, and I'll never do it again!'

'Scandalous! Scandalous! I never heard of such a thing!' said Mr. Growser.

'And where is this artist-gentleman now?' the Mayor asked.

'Oh, sir, when I saw him last he was going to Mrs. Goose's shop to have one of her sixpenny teas. You see, he's most awfully fond of cream buns. I expect he's still there.'

'But that must have been several hours ago,' the Mayor pointed out.

'Oh, yes, sir; but you can eat as many cakes as you like for sixpence at Mrs. Goose's,' replied Larry.

'I consider the whole thing to be a most disgraceful affair,' said the Mayor sternly.

'That's the first sensible thing you've said to-day, sir,' cried

57

Mr. Growser. 'It is. Disgraceful.'

'Oh, Mr. Mayor, sir, I'll never do it again.' Larry bleated. 'But I'm a very small lamb, and I didn't know any better. And it seemed a splendid idea.'

Then Ernest the policeman spoke. 'It was nothing more nor less than a swindle, in plain words, my lad. And as an officer of the law it will be my painful duty to take the names and addresses of every one concerned. You, being a young lamb and not knowing no better, and having confessed as it were, will be let off with a caution. And my advice to you, my lad, is to run round the streets and warn all your friends to pack up their pictures quick. Because if they don't there's going to be a big bonfire in the Square to-night. I'm now a-going round to Mrs. Goose's tea-shop to find this here artist.'

'And I shall not have a portrait of myself to hang in the Town Hall after all,' said the Mayor.

Mr. Growser thumped the floor with his umbrella. 'That is the only thing about the whole affair which we have to be thankful for!' he said.

The Arkville Dragon

SOME distance from Toytown, and away to the right as one travels by coach towards Arkville, lies a dense forest. Seen from the top of the coach it appears very dark and mysterious; strange-looking birds occasionally rise above the trees, curious rumblings are sometimes heard proceeding from the depths of the forest, and often travellers on the coach nudge each other and point to where, above the foliage, pencils of mist rise like smoke from hidden fires.

The only persons who ever go into the forest are the woodcutters, and they do not venture far, for one never knows what one might meet in a forest of that description.

One day the coach was rolling briskly along the Arkville road; upon the roof sat Larry the lamb and his friend Dennis the dachshund, for animals are not allowed to ride inside the coach. The aged driver turned to them and pointed with his whip towards the forest.

'They *do* say that away over there lives a dragon; nobody's ever seen it, but I remember when I was a boy there was a lot of talk about a dragon. They used to say that the smoke you could see was the dragon breathing.'

'It must be a very old dragon by this time,' remarked Larry.

'Old!' cried the driver, 'what do you mean, old?'

'Well, you said he was there when you were a boy,' replied Larry. 'And that must be a long time ago. He must be very

59

The aged driver pointed towards the forest

feeble by this time.'

'Feeble!' cried the driver. 'Here, you mind what you're saying, my lamb. You animals have too much to say for yourselves! I ain't as young as I was, I know, but that ain't no reason for you to start making rude remarks. There ain't many people what could drive this coach as careful as I can.'

'Oh, no, of course not,' said Larry hastily. 'Of course, everyone knows that you're not a bit old. But I expect the dragon was grown up when you were small. He couldn't have been a little boy dragon then, else he wouldn't have breathed smoke.'

'And why not?' asked the driver. 'Why shouldn't a little boy dragon breathe smoke?'

'Well, everyone knows that only grown-up people smoke. Little boys are not allowed to. It makes them sick. My friend Toby tried to buy cigarettes, and they wouldn't serve him.'

60

'But you don't understand,' said the driver. 'Dragons don't smoke cigarettes; they smoke natural-like. It's their breath that smokes, they're all hot inside.'

'Like when you swallow a mouthful of very hot tapioca?' Larry suggested.

'Oh, much hotter than that,' replied the driver. 'So hot, their breath is, that you can't go near them. That's what makes it so difficult to kill dragons. And that's why knights always put on armour when they go after dragons; it protects them from the hot breath.'

'Have you ever seen a dragon?' Larry asked.

'I haven't what you might call actually *seen* one,' the driver admitted. 'But I know what they look like. They're very long things, just like your friend Dennis there, only more so. If he hadn't got those long, floppy years, and had wings and horns, and was green-coloured instead of brown, he might easily be mistook for a dragon. Only, of course, dragons are bigger. But mark my words; one day everybody will see a dragon, because why? Because he'll get tired of being in that forest all by himself, and he'll come out to see where he is. And then that great fat policeman of ours will have to get to work and catch him.' He broke into a shrill laugh. 'I'd like to see policeman Ernest trying to catch a dragon; better than the theatre it would be!'

Just then the coach rattled into the square at Arkville, and pulled up before the sweet-stuff shop. Larry and Dennis climbed down, and then Dennis, who had been listening silently to the conversation on the coach, spoke:

'That's all nonsense about dragons. That driver is a silly old man. If he had seen the book I had in my sock last Christmas, he would know there are no such things as dragons. The book said so. It had a picture of a dragon with a knight fighting it; and underneath the picture it said the dragon was nothing but imagination.'

61

'What's imagination?' Larry asked.

'Something that you think is, but really isn't,' Dennis explained.

'Oh,' said Larry.

'But I an idea have got,' Dennis continued. 'I expect a lot of people don't know that a dragon all in the imagination is because not many people that book have seen. I don't expect Ernest the policeman has.'

'Ernest had a whistle in his sock last Christmas,' remarked Larry, 'not a book. He told me so.'

'Then I expect he doesn't know about there being no such things as dragons,' said Dennis. 'And that's why I an idea have. You see, Ernest has been to me very rude. He a sausage dog called me, just because I'm very long. Though, of course, it's very fashionable to be long and graceful.'

'It certainly *sounds* very rude,' Larry agreed.

'About that rude remark I've been thinking ever since,' said Dennis, 'and all this talk about dragons has this splendid idea given me.'

'Yes, but what *is* the idea?' Larry asked.

'Bend down,' said Dennis. 'I want to whisper.'

      ★   ★   ★   ★   ★

The police station, Toytown, stands in a street just off the square, and within easy reach of the Town Hall. It is a small, red building with a blue light outside, and over the door is a long white board with the word 'Police' painted upon it. Before the window of the police station stands another board upon which are pasted lists of lost umbrellas and other property, and descriptions of desperate characters for whose arrest rewards are offered. These descriptions often include portraits drawn by Ernest, who is a conscientious policeman, and spares no trouble.

One morning he sat in his little office. It was rather dark on account of the notice-board before the window, and round the

62

Toytown Police Station

walls ran shelves stacked with dozens and dozens of notebooks containing names and addresses which Ernest had taken in the course of his duties. Now he was bent over a sheet of paper, his tongue out and his helmet tilted back. He was drawing a picture of a highwayman for the notice-board.

Suddenly there came a clatter of hoofs, and into the police station dashed Larry the lamb.

'Oh, sir; oh, Mr. Ernest, sir!' he cried.

'What is it *now*?' asked Ernest, looking up. 'Can't you see I'm busy? Oh, it's you, is it? I never saw such a lamb for dashing about and running in and out, and disturbing people.'

'Oh, Mr. Ernest, sir,' cried Larry. 'I'm sorry to wake you, but I must tell you.'

'Wake me!' said Ernest. 'But I wasn't asleep. I never have time to sleep. What an idea! I was just finishing this picture of a highwayman I am after, so that people will known him when they meet him.'

'Is it like him?' Larry asked, peering at the drawing.

'I've never seen him, but it must be,' said Ernest. 'I've given him a mask—that black thing is the mask—and a cocked hat; and highwaymen always wear masks and cocked hats. And there's his horse in the background. That's the horse; prancing, he is.'

'Why has it only got two legs?' Larry inquired.

'Don't be silly,' replied the policeman. 'Two of the legs are in front of the other two. Horses always look like that in pictures. That's art, that is. And now, what do you want?'

'Oh, sir,' cried Larry. 'There's an awful great big dragon running about in the Arkville Road.'

'A great big what-er?' asked Ernest.

'A dragon,' Larry repeated. 'He's come out of the forest where he used to live. And he's breathing smoke. Do you know what it's like to have your mouth full of very hot tapioca pudding?'

64

'No, I never eat tapioca. Horrid stuff. Why? has the dragon got his mouth full of pudding?'

'Oh, no, sir; but he breathes like that, only hotter. Oh, Mr. Ernest, sir, don't you think you ought to see about it?'

'How do you know all this?' Ernest asked.

'Well, Mr. Ernest, it was like this. Yesterday I went to Arkville with my friend Dennis. Mrs. Goose had given me threepence for minding her shop while she went to the theatre. So I said to Dennis. "Let's go to Arkville." Because, you see, I had a penny each for the coach fare and a penny to spend on sweets when we got there.'

'I don't want to hear all your private affairs, you know,' said Ernest.

'No, sir, of course not. Well, we went. And on the way the driver of the coach told us all about a dreadful great dragon that lived in the forest. He's known about it for years.'

'The driver of that coach is a silly old man,' Ernest interrupted.

'Yes, that's what we thought. Well, when we got to Arkville we bought as many sweets as we could for a penny, and then we started to walk back to Toytown. Because, you see, I only had threepence. And just as we were passing the forest we heard an awful roaring, and a funny sizzling noise like a kettle makes when it boils over. And there was the dragon rolling its eyes, and flapping its wings, and twitching its horns. So we both ran. And Dennis said to me: "We must notify the police"—meaning I must tell you. And then he gave me this picture, out of a book, showing how to fight a dragon which, he thought, might be useful to you. There was something written under the picture; but Dennis seems to have torn that off.'

'Ah, that's a very useful picture,' said Ernest. 'Of course, everyone knows you must have armour to fight dragons in, but I might have forgotten it without the picture. You have done quite right, lamb, to tell me about this dragon. I shall proceed

65

'A suit of armour!' cried the Mayor

to arrest him as soon as I can make the necessary arrangements. You can rest easy in your bed, or your manger, or wherever you sleep, my lamb; the police have the matter in hand.'

A short time later Ernest the policeman was shown in to the Mayor's study at the Town Hall.

'Mr. Mayor, sir,' he said, 'I regret to have to say as how the Town will have to spend some money. A certain expense has arose—arisen—in connection with my duties as you might say. I require a suit of armour.'

'A suit of armour!' cried the Mayor. 'Did you say armour?'

'Armour,' repeated Ernest firmly.

'But I never heard of such a thing!' the Mayor cried. 'Whoever heard of a policeman going on his beat in armour. It's—it's ridiculous; and most unsuitable. You expect too much, officer. Just because you received a tin medal you are beginning to forget yourself. Armour indeed; you'll want a gold chain next.'

'I require only armour, your worship, in which to perform my duty. I have to arrest a very desperate character; I hope I know my duty, but I consider myself too valuable to the Town to attempt to do it in my blue uniform. The desperate character referred to is nothing more nor less than a dragon.'

'A dragon!' cried the Mayor. 'I didn't know we had any dragons about here; I'm sure I've never seen one. I should have noticed it particularly.'

'From information received, I gather that this one has just come out of the forest. It's very fierce and ferocious. It's a-gallivanting about on the Arkville road a-breathing hot tap—hot smoke, and being a danger to peaceful travellers. Knowing my duty as I do, I'm a-going to arrest that dragon. I want a suit of armour to do it in, and I want it quick.'

'You shall have it, officer; you shall have it. You are a brave fellow. Of course, now, I understand the position . . . I will give you a note for the Inventor; he will fit you out, I'm sure. Call on me for anything else you require. You will want a horse for one

67

thing; take one of the coach horses. Come and see me before you go. And if—that is to say when—you return I have no doubt the Town will feel inclined to present you with some slight mark of esteem, such as a new silver whistle or—or something.'

'Thank you, your worship,' replied Ernest. 'That will be something to look forward to.'

★   ★   ★   ★   ★

The news of the dragon spread through the Town like wildfire, and when it became known that Ernest the policeman was boldly setting out to arrest the creature a large crowd collected in front of the Town Hall to see him off. He appeared on the steps enclosed in bright tin armour, and walked down into the square with a loud clanking and clattering. A cheer went up.

Ernest seemed to find his armour very awkward and he looked hot and uncomfortable; but he bowed in a dignified manner to the crowd and then walked to the horse which awaited him and beside which stood the Mayor.

'You see, your worship, I am wearing my armlet,' said Ernest, 'so that although I am all dressed up like this people can still see I'm an officer of the law on duty.'

'Quite right, officer, quite right,' replied the Mayor. 'Very proper.'

'And this here chain is to fasten round the dragon's neck. I thought very likely the handcuffs wouldn't fit.'

'Splendid,' said the Mayor. You think of everything. And now I have a suggestion to offer. I have been thinking the matter over and reading some books on dragons and hunting, and so on. And it occurs to me that when the dragon sees you he may retreat into the forest and hide; and that would be very inconvenient. But it appears that dragons are very fond of sheep, and if you took a sheep with you the dragon would probably be tempted to come and sniff at it; then you could arrest him without difficulty. Well, we haven't any sheep, but

68

we have a very public-spirited lamb.'

And he pointed to Larry, who had just wriggled his way into the front rank of the crowd.

'Ha! Larry!' said Ernest. 'Where is your friend Dennis to-day?'

'He's—he's busy,' Larry stammered.

'Busy, is he? And how is it you're looking so untidy? You've got green paint all over your fleece. You've been messing about with paint pots, I'll be bound.'

'I'll try to be brave,' said Larry

'Paint?' said Larry. 'Why, it does look something like paint, doesn't it? That's funny; I wonder how it got there.'

'Now, Larry, my lamb,' said the Mayor. 'Never mind the paint. Are you prepared to accompany our brave policeman and tempt the dragon?'

'Oh, sir! Oh, sir!' Larry bleated; 'I don't think I could do that. I don't think I could tempt a dragon. Besides, I'm very timid. All lambs are timid.'

69

'You would be quite safe,' Ernest pointed out. 'I should be there to protect you. The dragon would only sniff at you; I shouldn't let him start nibbling.'

'And think of the honour and glory!' cried the Mayor.

'Oh, yes; of course, sir. But I don't *really* think I should be much help. And it might be very—very awkward!'

'Nonsense,' the Mayor said. 'Then that is quite settled.'

'Very well, sir, if you say I must I suppose I must. I'll try to be brave. But if I run away when I see the dragon you must

Out of the trees dashed a long green object

excuse me. And don't hurt the dragon, Mr. Ernest.'

'I shall not hurt him,' Ernest replied, 'unless he gets very ferocious; in which case it will be my duty to give him a smart rap over the head with my truncheon. As for running away, I am going to tie this rope round your neck so you can't.'

Then Ernest fastened the rope to Larry, mounted his horse

70

and, amidst the cheers of the crowd, rode clanking out of the square with Larry trotting behind. Along the Arkville Road they went, the policeman's armour clattering and Larry's little hoofs padding behind in the dust; and at last they reached the edge of the forest. Ernest looked cautiously about him and then suddenly pulled up his horse with a jerk.

'There he is!' he shouted.

Out of the trees dashed a long green object. It seemed to have horns and little wings which flapped, and it leapt about in the middle of the roadway and made a noise very like a bark.

'Why, it's only a baby dragon!' cried Ernest. 'And it barks. I never knew dragons barked before. Come along then, dragon; I won't hurt you.' And he made a chirruping noise.

'Yap, yap!' said the dragon.

'There, there!' said Ernest. 'Come along then!'

The dragon gave another bark and jumped back amongst the trees. Ernest immediately climbed down from his horse and ran clumsily after it into the forest, while Larry sat down by the roadside and listened to the sounds of the chase. He heard barking, and the shouts of Ernest, and the clatter of Ernest's armour and, as far as he could judge, the baby dragon appeared to be having quite a game with his pursuer. But then Larry's eyes grew round with astonishment; a loud roaring suddenly arose in the forest.

The horse looked at Larry and spoke. 'I don't like this; I'm going home.' And, turning, he trotted back towards Toytown.

The roaring grew louder, and then from between the trees rushed the baby dragon. One of its wings had come off and was hanging by a piece of string, its horns had gone and it looked very frightened.

'There's a real one!' he shouted breathlessly. 'Run!' And he, too, set off towards Toytown at full speed.

But Larry was too overcome to run; he stood there with his little hoofs clattering with fright. With a roar and a crashing of

71

branches a large green dragon jumped out on to the roadway; round its neck was a chain, and hanging on to the other end of the chain was Ernest the policeman.

'I've got him,' he cried. 'Don't be alarmed; he's not a bit fierce, only nervous. Come and catch hold of this chain and lend me a hand. There, there, dragon; it's all right. I shan't hurt you.'

'Oh Mr. Ernest, sir, I don't think I had better come too close,' said Larry. 'Not after what the Mayor said about dragons liking sheep. I'll run on to Toytown and tell them you are coming.'

★   ★   ★   ★   ★

A crowd was assembled in the square at Toytown anxiously awaiting the policeman's return when Larry came clattering over the cobble-stones, waving his front hoofs and shouting.

'He's got him!' he bleated. 'Mr. Ernest has caught the dragon! Where is the Mayor? Tell the Mayor!'

'Here I am, my lamb,' said the Mayor. 'Now, take your time; take your time. Do I understand that the constable has arrested the dragon?'

'Oh, yes, sir!' cried Larry. 'He's arrested it. With his chain. He's bringing it along now; he'll be here in a minute.'

'Ha! A very competent officer,' said the Mayor. 'Very competent indeed.'

'Here he is!' shouted the crowd, and began to cheer.

Into the square marched Ernest the policeman leading the dragon behind him. The dragon appeared to be quite tame and trotted along behind Ernest, its tail curled over its back and its tongue hanging out. It stopped and hesitated when it saw the crowd, but Ernest made a chirruping noise to encourage it, and the dragon allowed itself to be led forward towards the Mayor.

'I have to report dragon duly arrested,' said Ernest, saluting. 'This is it. It was very desperate at first, but has now quieted down as you can see.'

72

'What is it *now*?' asked Ernest (*page 64*)

'I require a suit of armour,' said Ernest (*page 67*)

'Why, its only a baby dragon!' cried Ernest, 'and it barks' *(page 71)*

With a roar and a crashing of branches, a large green dragon jumped out *(page 71)*

Into the square marched Ernest leading the dragon behind him
(*page 72*)

Dennis the Dachshund was sticky with green paint and asked, 'is it safe to come out?' (*page 74*)

'Splendid!' said the Mayor. 'You have done well, officer. We shall not forget it. But I cannot help feeling that the creature is a trifle disappointing. For one thing its breath is not at all fiery; not even smoky. And it is not as large as I had expected. But still you can't be blamed for that. I wonder whether it likes milk.'

'Oh, sir, shall I fetch it a saucer of milk?' Larry asked.

'Bring some milk by all means,' said the Mayor. 'But bring it in a pail.'

When the milk arrived the dragon lapped it up eagerly and then wagged its tail for more. Several townspeople then came forward and offered it carrots, buns and pieces of sugar, all of which the dragon took. It appeared to be hungry.

'And now,' said the Mayor, 'the question arises: what are we going to do with the creature? You can't keep it in the police station, and it is too big for a kennel.'

'I thought of that coming along, your worship,' Ernest replied, 'and it seems to me the best thing we can do with it is to present it to Mr. Noah. No doubt it would soon settle down with the other animals, and very likely Mr. Noah could teach it to beg. And now, your worship, I have other duties to attend to if you will excuse me. I must get the Inventor to remove this armour; it's all soldered on and I can't get to my pockets. Larry, my lad; I want a word with you.'

'Yes, sir; certainly, Mr. Ernest,' said Larry nervously. And he followed the policeman round the corner.

'Now, my lamb,' Ernest continued, 'I seem to remember seeing something in the nature of a baby dragon over there by the forest.'

'That's funny,' replied Larry. 'I thought I saw one too.'

'Things having turned out satisfactory-like,' said Ernest, gazing sternly at Larry, 'and me likely to be presented with a silver whistle for my services, I am not prepared to inquire too closely into that matter of the baby dragon. But I have my

73

ideas!'

'Yes, sir,' Larry murmured, shifting from one hoof to the other.

'But,' Ernest went on. 'if you should happen to see a certain friend of yours whose name I need not mention, you may give him a hint. A joke's a joke (you can say) but playing practical jokes on the police is trifling with the law, and a very serious matter. Many a person has had his name and address took for less. And in case you don't know it let me tell you, my lad, that to assist the practical joker in any way whatsoever—such as telling the police what isn't true with intent to deceive—is also a very serious matter. We'll let it go at that. Good day to you, lamb.'

Larry scurried home to the barn where he lived, and there, as he had expected, lay Dennis the dachshund. He was hiding behind a barrel. He was sticky with green paint and his ears were tied back with string.

'Is it safe to come out?' he asked when he caught sight of Larry. 'Because, if so, I wish you would my ears untie and help to rub this paint off. I had an awful fright when I that dragon saw; I never thought there was a real dragon. Whoever would have thought that old coach-driver knew what he was talking about!'

'Let this be a lesson to you,' said Larry severely. 'It is very wrong to play jokes on the police; I can see that now. You might have been eaten by that dragon, and then you would only have had yourself to blame. It would have served you right. And it would have served me right, too, for telling all those awful stories to Mr. Ernest. I'll never do it again.'

'We a lucky escape have had,' Dennis admitted. 'But, after all, a splendid idea it was.'

The Toytown Treasure

HALF-WAY down Ark street, and not far from the Theatre Royal, stands the house of Mr. Growser. It is a two-storied building, rather dark and dirty-looking, the woodwork badly needing a coat of paint, and the windows grimy and cracked.

Although Mr. Growser is said to be very rich, he is rather mean and dislikes spending money on such uninteresting things as paint and glass.

One afternoon there came a timid knock at the front door, and when, after a good deal of grumbling, Mr. Growser opened it, there upon the step stood the small figure of Larry the lamb. He looked very neat and trim; his hoofs were brightly polished, and the wool on top of his head had been parted in the middle. A wooden tray hung from his shoulders by a strap, and between his hoofs he held a tin with a slot cut in the top. When the door opened Larry rattled the contents of the tin vigorously and bleated:

'Oh, sir; oh, sir!'

'This is disgraceful!' cried the old gentleman. 'Banging on my door just when I am about to take my afternoon nap, and then rattling a tin at me!'

'Oh, sir; oh, please, sir——' said Larry.

'You ought to be ashamed of yourself,' shouted Mr. Growser. 'Go away; go away!'

'Oh, but, sir; I haven't finished.'

'Finished! I should hope not indeed. You ought never to

have begun. Rattling a tin like that; it ought not to be allowed!'

'Oh, sir,' cried Larry. 'Will you please buy a flag?'

'A flag! Did I hear you say a flag? I never heard such impudence. Do I look like the sort of person who would run about waving flags!'

'Oh, no, sir, you don't,' replied Larry. 'But you need not wave it; you just stick it in your buttonhole. They're only a penny each.'

'Ha, indeed! And why should I give you a penny for a piece of paper with a pin stuck through it? Eh? Answer me that!'

'Oh, sir, it's for a very noble cause,' Larry bleated. 'Awfully noble. It's for the Home for Destitute Lambs.'

'And where may that be?' asked Mr. Growser.

'It's in Mr. Giles' barn,' said Larry. 'Until we find a more comfortable place. And every penny you give helps to keep a destitute lamb.'

'But I was not aware there were any destitute lambs about here. In fact, you are the only lamb I have ever seen in Toytown. How many are in your home, eh? Answer me that, animal.'

'Only one, sir, at present,' replied Larry. 'But I am sure there must be a lot about if I could only find them.'

'Ha, it's a trick!' cried the old gentleman. 'I thought so; disgraceful! Disgraceful! You come here asking for a penny, and all the time it's a trick to enrich yourself. You ought to be ashamed!'

'Well, will you buy a flag sir?' asked Larry, rattling his tin.

'Get off my step!' shouted Mr. Growser. 'Take yourself off. I wonder you can look me in the face, let alone rattle a tin in front of it. Be off, or I'll send for the policeman!'

'What's all this?' said a deep voice. Larry turned to find Ernest the policeman standing just behind him; and he jumped so violently that he upset all his flags on Mr. Growser's door-step.

'It's disgraceful, that's what it is!' said the old gentleman. 'Disgraceful. Here's this animal rattling a tin and bleating, and now he's upset all these paper flags on my doorstep. He ought to be made to pick them up.'

'Oh, sir, I'm sorry, but I can't,' cried Larry. 'You see, my little hoofs are so awkward for picking things up. Perhaps you and Mr. Ernest would pick them up for me.'

Still grumbling, Mr. Growser stooped and began to gather up the paper flags, and Ernest the policeman pulled off his white gloves to help. But suddenly the old gentleman paused and looked very hard at the flags; then he looked very hard at Larry; and then at Ernest the policeman.

'How much are you asking for these flags, Larry, my lamb?' Mr. Growser asked. 'A penny each, did you say? I will give you sixpence for the whole lot.'

'Here, what's all this?' asked Ernest in surprise. 'It ain't like you, Mr. Growser, to be offering sixpence for some bits of paper.'

'It's for a very noble cause,' said Mr. Growser.

Ernest bent down and stared at the flags, and then he, too, looked very hard at Larry, and then at Mr. Growser.

'Where did you get this here paper, Larry, my lad?' Ernest asked.

'Oh, sir, I found it in the Magician's dustbin,' replied Larry. 'And I cut it up with Mr. Giles' scissors and then stuck pins through the pieces.'

'And did you read what was on the back of the paper before you cut it up, my lad?' Ernest inquired.

'Oh, no, sir; I didn't trouble,' said Larry.

'I'll give you ninepence for the lot,' cried Mr. Growser.

'No, you won't, Mr. Growser, sir; nor yet tenpence nor a shilling neither,' said Ernest. 'This here paper what's been cut up so careless-like looks to me like a very important document. I can see quite plain on one bit 'Where the treasure is hid,' and

77

'What's all this?' said a deep voice

on another bit I can see what looks like part of a plan or map. And there's a lot of figures and letters what will have to be put together and read careful. It is my duty to take charge of this document. Larry, my lad, you will come with me to the Town Hall along with these bits of paper you've been and cut up so careless.'

'Eighteen pence!' cried Mr. Growser.

'No, Mr. Growser, sir. Nor yet one and fivepence. I hope I know my duty. This document goes to the Town Hall. If there's any treasure buried in Toytown it is the property of the town. Have you got any of those flags in your hand? Give them here, Mr. Growser. I don't want any jiggery-pokery with you.'

Ernest carefully collected every piece of paper and then took Larry by the hoof. 'Come along, my lad,' he said. 'We'll go and see the Mayor.'

'Half a crown!' shouted the old gentleman after them.

'Oh, Mr. Ernest, sir,' sir said Larry. 'Half a crown is a lot of money. I could buy an awful lot of lollipops with half a crown.'

'Don't you worry, my lad,' replied Ernest. 'If this document is what I think it is I wouldn't be a bit surprised if you get a very handsome reward.'

'Much more than half a crown?' Larry asked.

'Much more,' said Ernest. 'If this leads to the recovery of buried treasure I wouldn't be a bit surprised if you get five shillings—at least.'

★   ★   ★   ★   ★

When Ernest arrived with Larry at the Town Hall and told his story to the Mayor, that gentleman listened with great interest, and even put aside the game of noughts and crosses upon which he had been engaged in order that the pieces of paper might be spread out upon his table.

'This seems to be a very important matter,' said the Mayor. 'And evidently a most important paper this lamb has cut up. He ought to be more careful.'

'Oh, Mr. Mayor, sir, I didn't know any better,' cried Larry. 'You see, I'm only a little lamb, and when I saw that dirty old paper in the Magician's dustbin I thought it would make splendid flags. And it was for a very noble cause.'

'He was a-selling the flags for a home for destitute lambs, your worship,' remarked Ernest. 'It sounds to me like a swindle seeing as how he's the only lamb in the town. If I hadn't been sharp he might have sold the flags before I found out how important it was.'

'But is this lamb destitute, officer?' the Mayor asked.

'I wouldn't be surprised, your worship. I thought he looked a bit funny when I saw him yesterday.'

'You don't seem to understand the meaning of the word 'destitute,' officer. It means without any money. Have you no money, my lamb?'

'Oh, no, sir. I spent the last of my pocket-money yesterday. And I read the word 'destitute' in a book, and thought what a nice, long word it sounded.'

'If you'll pardon me saying so, your worship,' said Ernest, 'instead of talking about long words what nobody knows the meaning of, we ought to be looking into this matter of the treasure. Let's spread out these bits of paper and see if we can make them fit.'

'That's an idea, certainly,' the Mayor agreed. 'Though I will trouble you to speak rather more respectfully when addressing your mayor.'

Ernest and the Mayor fumbled with the pieces of paper for some time, while Larry stood on the tips of his hoofs and watched. It did not take very long to arrange the pieces because Larry had been unable to use the scissors very well, and the edges were so uneven that it was fairly easy to see where the joins should come. And at last all the pieces had been fitted together and the Mayor was able to read the entire paper.

'Ha, you were perfectly right, officer,' he said. 'It *is* about

80

'Oh, sir,' cried Larry, 'would you please buy a flag?' (*page 76*)

Ernest arrived with Larry and told his story to the Mayor (*page 79*)

'You ought to be ashamed to make such a noise,' shouted Mr Growser (*page 85*)

'Here, who done that?' cried Ernest (*page 92*)

buried treasure. This is very important; very important indeed. Listen; I will read it to you:

'How to Find the Buried Treasure.
'1, 2, 3, 4, 5, 6, 7. Everybody can see it. A lot of people would rather not. 8, 9, 10. When you come to it take six steps to the right (or left as the case may be) and mind the step. 11, 12, 13, 14, 15. Go as far as you can if he isn't there, and dig in the middle or blow up, if preferred. It's in a black box if somebody has not been there first. Signed, Joe Higgins, gentleman.'

'Is that all, sir?' Ernest asked. 'Because if so all I can say is that it don't make sense. Not nohow, it don't.'
'Of course it doesn't make sense, officer,' said the Mayor. 'How unreasonable you are. Whoever heard of a guide to buried treasure making sense? If it did anyone could understand it. It's supposed to be mysterious; a sort of riddle or puzzle.'
'Then what's the good of writing it down at all, that's what I want to know? Silly I call it. The only thing I understand about it is the name. I remember Joe Higgins, gentleman. Gentleman of the road, he was; a highwayman, in plain language. Many's the time I've arrested him. The last time he escaped, and I haven't seen him since.'
'Then you can depend upon it, officer, that this treasure consists of the watches and other articles stolen by this highwayman. We must solve the puzzle, officer. Pull yourself together now; pull yourself together. Use your wits. What, for example, do you make of these numbers?'
'Oh, sir, I know!' Larry bleated. 'They're put in to make it more difficult.'
'A very shrewd remark, my lamb. A very shrewd remark. I think you are very probably right. Now, officer; let us ignore the numbers and consider carefully the rest of the message.

Larry scampered out into the square

"Everybody can see it." What do you make of that?'

'I don't make nothing of it at all, your worship. Not nohow, I don't. Nonsense it sounds to me.'

'Remember, officer, the next sentence. "A lot of people would rather not see it." What can it be?'

'Well your worship, the only thing I can think of what everybody can see, and a lot of people don't want to see, is your statue in the middle of the square.'

'I beg your pardon, officer,' said the Mayor in a slow, distinct voice.

'Well, so it is, your worship. I says what I means, I does. Going about my beat I hear things what I'm not meant to hear. Only yesterday I heard a person say out loud in front of your statue as how it looked like something a cat had been gnawing. I took his name and address prompt. I hope I know my duty.'

'You were quite right, officer; quite right. I hope it will prove a warning to other criminals. But to return to this matter of the buried treasure. As I am so expert at cross-word puzzles (to say nothing of noughts and crosses), I have no doubt I shall soon be able to solve the mystery; but I must be left alone. I cannot solve a puzzle of this kind while you, officer, are breathing heavily at my elbow and this lamb is scraping his hoofs against my chair. Go away, both of you.'

Larry and Ernest left the Mayor, and Larry scampered out into the square. And, to his surprise, there stood Mr. Growser leaning on his stick, looking rather more disagreeable than usual, and staring hard at the statue of the Mayor which stood before the Town Hall. As soon as he caught sight of Larry he beckoned, and then led the way into a side street.

'Well, lamb,' he said. 'Have you considered my offer?'

'Oh, Mr. Growser, sir,' bleated Larry, 'I should love to sell you all my flags for five shillings——'

'Half a crown, animal, half a crown. Do you suppose I should give you five shillings? I never heard of such a thing.

83

You ought to be ashamed to suggest it.'

'I mean half a crown sir,' replied Larry. 'I would take half a crown for the flags, but I haven't got them any longer. The Mayor has them, and he's stuck them all together and we've read the writing on the back. It's about buried treasure, and the Mayor is working out the puzzle now.'

'Ah, it's a pity he hasn't something else to do. Disgraceful I call it. And did you read the writing?'

'Oh, yes, sir; I read it,' replied Larry. 'Several times.'

Mr Growser calls on the Inventor in his workshop

'Ha! then I suppose you can remember it? Very well then. Now, I said I would give you half a crown for the pieces of paper; and so that you shall not feel disappointed I will give you a shilling—one shilling— if you can remember the writing.'

'Oh, yes, Mr. Growser, sir; I can remember it quite well. Where is the shilling?'

'But you must repeat the thing to me,' said the old gentleman. 'Else how am I to know you do remember it?'

So Larry recited the contents of the document in a little

84

bleating voice (leaving out the numbers, however), while Mr. Growser listened attentively. Then Mr. Growser asked Larry to say it all over again; after which he gave Larry the promised shilling, and turning round, began hobbling away as fast as he could go.

*   *   *   *   *

The Inventor stood at a bench in his workshop beating a sheet of tin with a heavy hammer. The noise he made was terrific, and it is not surprising, therefore, that he did not hear the sound of footsteps as Mr. Growser cautiously entered the room and came towards him, thumping the floor with his stick at every step.

'This is disgraceful!' shouted Mr. Growser. 'You ought to be ashamed to make such a noise. It ought not to be allowed.'

'Ah, it's you, Mr. Growser, is it?' said the Inventor, laying down his hammer. 'And what can I do for you? You haven't come to see my new beetle-killer by any chance?'

'Certainly not,' cried the old gentleman, 'I have no wish to see a beetle-killer.'

'But it's a very novel beetle-killer,' the Inventor pointed out. 'And extremely simple. It works with treacle.'

'I don't like treacle,' shouted Mr. Growser, banging the floor with his stick. 'I don't like beetles, either; I don't like anything. I don't like the noise you are always making, and I shouldn't be here now if I hadn't a little piece of work for you.'

'Perhaps you are not worried by beetles?' the Inventor suggested.

'I'm worried by everything and everybody,' cried Mr. Growser. 'I don't suppose there was ever a man who was as worried and annoyed by everything as I am. Now, come, sir, forget your beetle trap and pay attention. I understand you invent things.'

'Yes, I've invented quite a lot of things. Quite a lot. For example——'

'And I suppose you are good at puzzling things out?'

'Yes, quite good. I've had to puzzle out a lot of things. For example——'

'Are you capable of solving a riddle?'

'A riddle? Really, Mr. Growser, I hope you haven't interrupted my work to ask me riddles?'

'Talk sense, sir. You ought to be ashamed of yourself suggesting such a thing! When I say riddles I mean a puzzle; a mysterious message. I have here a sheet of paper on which I have written down a curious message exactly as it was repeated to me. I wish you to solve it. I expect to pay a fee, of course; expense is no object. That is, within reason. I do not wish to go beyond two and sixpence.'

The Inventor took the paper and read it carefully. Then he looked up at Mr. Growser.

'This concerns a buried treasure,' he said. 'You can hardly expect me to puzzle this out for a mere half-crown. I will solve it for you with pleasure, but I must insist upon a half-share of the treasure. You see, you can't read it without my help, and also it looks as though you will have to blow something up. Now, I am rather good at blowing up things; none better, though I say it myself. In fact, I have just invented a new sort of gunpowder, which will be excellent for this purpose.'

'You ought to be ashamed of yourself!' cried Mr. Growser. 'A half-share indeed. You are a thoroughly grasping fellow. I wonder you can look me in the face. However, I suppose I shall have to agree because, as you say, your gunpowder may be necessary. Now, sir, don't stand here arguing. Get to work; get to work. Solve the puzzle.'

'For a half-share?' asked the Inventor.

'Yes, sir; a half-share. Though I have said before, and I will say again, that you ought to be ashamed of yourself.'

'Very good,' said the Inventor. 'Now, let me see; "Everybody can see it; a lot of people would rather not." What would

86

that be?'

'The stage coach,' replied the old gentleman.

'Why the stage coach?'

'Because it is a disgrace to Toytown. It ought not to be allowed. Of all the slow, unwieldly, badly managed conveyances——'

'No. The stage coach is not the object referred to. Remember that this message was written by a highwayman. Now, what is it a highwayman would rather not see?'

'Don't ask me, sir. Don't ask me. If I am to give you half the treasure for solving this puzzle, solve it. Don't expect me to do it.'

'The police station,' replied the Inventor. 'Obvious. I wonder you didn't think of it. Now, "When you come to it take six steps to the right (or the left as the case may be) and mind the step." Obviously this refers to the way from which you approach the police station. If you come from one end of the street you would turn right; if from the other end you would naturally turn to the left. Quite obvious. Don't you agree?'

'Don't ask me, sir. Don't ask me. I know nothing about police stations. I don't approve of police stations. I believe in prisons where people, who are a nuisance to everybody, can be locked up.'

' "Go as far as you can, " ' the inventor continued, ' "if he isn't there." Who isn't there?'

'Don't ask me, sir. Are you solving this puzzle or am I?'

'Quite obvious,' said the the Inventor. 'It refers to the policeman. Quite sensible too; what I mean, one could hardly dig for treasure in the police station with the policeman about. Now: "Dig in the middle or blow up as preferred. It's in a black box if somebody has not been there first." Well, it all seems quite clear; I wonder you couldn't understand it yourself. All we have to do now is to take round a barrel of my new gunpowder and blow up the police station. When the smoke has cleared

'*I suppose your gunpowder won't blow up the town?*'

away no doubt we shall find the treasure quite easily.'

'I suppose you know your own business,' said Mr. Growser. 'but it seems extraordinary to me. Why should a highwayman bury his treasure in the police station?'

'Why not?' asked the inventor. 'It seems as good a place as any. After all, he must have spent a good deal of time in the police station. Being arrested by Ernest and all that. Perfectly simple to bury the treasure under the floor when Ernest was out on his beat. You may depend upon it, the treasure is there, Mr. Growser. We will go round after dark with a nice big barrel of gunpowder.'

'I suppose your gunpowder won't blow up the town by any chance? Is it very strong?'

'I don't know,' replied the Inventor. 'I haven't tried it yet.'

*   *   *   *   *

That evening, when most of the inhabitants of Toytown were at supper, the Mayor and Ernest the policeman might have been seen in the square near the Mayor's statue. The Mayor held in his hand the paper relating to the treasure, while Ernest had a spade and a yard-measure. The Mayor was taking long strides in one direction after another, while at every six steps he would close his eyes and count to himself.

'Well, your worship, have you solved the mystery?' Ernest asked.

'I feel sure I have, officer,' replied the Mayor. 'It is really quite simple, though I still have a little calculating to do. Are you any good at multiplication, officer?'

'Very fair, sir. I know up to twelve times, if that's any help.'

'Because I have decided, officer, that the lamb was wrong in supposing the figures in the document have been put in to deceive. It seems quite clear to me now that the figures contain the clue to the mystery; but a good deal of arithmetic is required.'

'Well, sir, arithmetic is all very well in its place, but what I

89

The Mayor was taking long strides in one direction after onother

want to know is: where is the treasure? Do you know, or don't
you? Because I've been messing about all day over this bit of
paper, and I've got some work to do at the police station.'

'Don't be so impatient, officer; don't be so impatient. I know
roughly where the treasure is, I feel sure. It only wants a little
thought. Now, where would a highwayman dig if he wanted to
bury something?'

Ernest replied promptly. 'In the ground, I should think, sir.'

'Exactly, officer. Just what I thought. But one can't dig
through cobble-stones, can one?'

'I can't, your worship,' replied Ernest. 'At least, I ain't
a-going to try. I have got to make out a description of a lost dog

90

to stick on my notice board.'

'Then go and do it,' cried the Mayor. 'Go and do it. I am quite capable of finding this treasure without your assistance. Go away, and leave the spade here. Also the yard-measure.'

'All right, sir; I will. And I hope you find the treasure. I *hopes* so; and I won't say no more. It ain't for me to say what I think. I know my duty. If you want me you'll find me in the police station; in the back office.'

Ernest hurried away, and for some time the Mayor worked on in silence; consulting the paper at intervals, counting on his fingers and occasionally taking long strides which he afterwards measured carefully. But suddenly there came an interruption. There was a bleating, a clatter of hoofs and into the square dashed Larry the lamb.

'Oh, sir! Oh, sir!' cried Larry.

'What is it, lamb? What is it?' said the Mayor testily. 'Can't you see I'm busy?'

'Oh, sir; oh, Mr. Mayor, sir!' Larry bleated.

'Take your time, my lamb. Take your time,' said the Mayor. 'Don't get flustered. Now, what is it?'

'Oh, Mr. Mayor, sir, I've just seen a dreadful thing. I've just seen Mr. Growser and the Inventor, and they were carrying a huge barrel.'

'A barrel. What was there dreadful in that?'

'Gunpowder was in it, sir,' Larry replied. 'It said on the barrel "Gunpowder. With care." '

'Gunpowder!' cried the Mayor.

'Oh, yes, sir; gunpowder. The stuff that goes bang. They put the barrel on the steps of the police station, and the Inventor asked me if I had a match. And I hadn't, and Mr. Growser hadn't either. So the Inventor went away to find some.'

'Good gracious!' cried the Mayor. 'This is terrible. Terrible. They're going to blow up the police station. And the constable is inside! You did quite right to tell me, my lamb. Quite right.

91

They were carrying a huge barrel!

Come, we must hurry to the police station. How fortunate the constable left the spade here. We shall be able to dig him out if we are too late to prevent the explosion.'

Shouldering the spade the Mayor hurried towards the police station, followed by Larry; but just as they came in sight of the building there was a loud bang, a clatter of breaking glass and the street became filled with smoke. Two heads were peering round the corner, and the Mayor was able to recognise Mr. Growser and the Inventor; but when they saw they were observed those two gentlemen turned and ran.

The smoke cleared away, and from the front window of the police station, from which all the glass had disappeared, there protruded the head of Ernest the policeman.

'Here, who done that?' cried Ernest. 'Who's been a-letting off fireworks on my doorstep?'

'Are you quite safe, officer?' the Mayor asked. 'You wouldn't like me to dig you out, or anything of that sort?'

'I'm safe enough, your worship,' Ernest replied. 'Except that my helmet was blown off. Blown clean off, it was. Who done it, that's what I want to know? I'll learn him whoever it was.'

'I am very much afraid it was Mr. Growser and the Inventor,' said the Mayor.

'Ah, Mr. Growser, was it?' cried Ernest. 'I thought he was annoyed with me for not letting him have that paper. This is his idea of revenge.'

'Oh, Mr. Mayor; Mr. Ernest,' Larry bleated. 'I expect they were after the treasure. It said on the paper, "blow up if preferred." I suppose they did prefer it.'

'Treasure!' said the Mayor. 'But how did they obtain a copy of the document. I understood, officer, that you were most particular in not allowing Mr. Growser to read the paper.'

'Oh, sir, I remember now; I told him,' said Larry. 'He asked me if I remembered what the paper was about, and I did. And he said he would give me a shilling if I really could remember, so I said it all over to show that I did. And he gave me the shilling. Perhaps Mr. Growser remembered what I said.'

'Scandalous!' cried the Mayor. 'Taking advantage of a young lamb like that! There is only one comfort; they have not found the treasure.'

'Treasure?' said a voice at the Mayor's elbow. And turning, the Mayor saw the Magician, who had come along the street unheard during the conversation.

'Did I hear you say treasure?' inquired the Magician. 'And are you referring, by any chance, to the treasure mentioned in an old sheet of paper of mine?'

'Well, ahem; yes,' the Mayor admitted, in rather a shamefaced manner. 'Now you mention it, I believe the paper was found in your dustbin.'

'And have you been blowing up the street to find it?' the Magician asked. 'Oh dear, dear, dear; that is really funny. You might have saved yourself a lot of trouble by coming to me first. I found that treasure weeks ago; that's why I threw the paper away. I had finished with it.'

'You found it!' cried the Mayor. 'Then you were able to read the puzzle?'

'Oh dear, no,' said the Magician. 'There was no need. You see, I saw the highwayman bury it. At the cross-roads it was, when I happened to be out looking for magic herbs. I watched him from behind a hedge, and when he had finished I made a mooing sound like a cow. And the fellow was so frightened he turned and ran. He dropped that paper and I picked it up. But, of course, I didn't trouble to puzzle it out. I just went home for a spade and dug the treasure up again.'

'How much was it?' cried Ernest and the Mayor together.

'Only one and sixpence and a large ball of silver paper,' the Magician replied. 'Hardly worth digging for. Good-night to you all. You need not trouble to return the document, Mr. Mayor. I have quite finished with it.'

When the Magician had gone the Mayor looked at Ernest, and Ernest looked at the Mayor.

'Then we've had our trouble for nothing.' said the Mayor. 'We are no better off than before; in fact, you are worse off, officer, for all your windows are broken.'

'Don't let that worry you, your worship,' replied the constable. 'Mr. Growser and the Inventor will pay for those, or I'll know the reason why. I'm a-going to look for those two gentlemen now.'

'And I suppose that you, my lamb, are going to spend the shilling Mr. Growser gave you,' the Mayor asked Larry.

'Oh, no, sir,' Larry bleated. 'I've spent that already. On lollipops. You can get an awful lot of lollipops for a shilling. And now I am going home to my barn. I'm feeling very funny inside, so I'm going to lie down in my manger. Perhaps I shan't feel quite so funny in the morning.'

The Disgraceful Business at Mrs Goose's

MRS.Goose kept the confectioner's shop near the Arkville Gate, Toytown. This was a convenient place for such a shop because every visitor from Arkville had to come through the gate and pass her window, which was always nicely set out with a collection of tempting cakes; and as Mrs. Goose supplied teas in addition to selling cakes and sweets, she obtained plenty of customers. Wednesday, which was early-closing time in Arkville, was a particularly busy time for Mrs. Goose; for on that afternoon cheap excursions from Arkville were run by the coach, and Mrs. Goose, who was quite a smart old lady, had a private arrangement with the coach-driver. She kept him supplied with an unlimited quantity of chewing-gum, and in consideration of this he always pulled up the coach just outside her shop, before proceeding to the Square, and mentioned to his passengers the excellence of Mrs. Goose's teas. And at last the time came when the old lady decided she must have assistance in the shop.

One Monday morning Larry the lamb and Dennis the dachshund were at the counter purchasing a pennyworth of sweets for which Larry was paying; for Dennis never appeared to have any money, and Larry seldom had much after Monday. And as Mrs. Goose served the animals and observed Larry's nice clean fleece and shiny hoofs, and his friend's sleek, brown coat, it occured to her that here were two very gentlemanly

95

'Would you like to work for me?' inquired Mrs Goose

animals who would make splendid shop-assistants.

'I wonder whether you two creatures would care to do a little work for me?' she inquired.

Larry looked at Dennis and Dennis looked at Larry. 'What sort of work?' Dennis asked cautiously.

'Well, you know how busy I am here,' said Mrs. Goose. 'All these people coming in from Arkville; and then his worship the Mayor often takes tea here because he is so fond of my cream buns, and Mr. Ernest the constable drops in sometimes. In fact, I keep a specially large breakfast-cup for Mr. Ernest. Then yesterday afternoon I had a crew of pirates here from a ship in the harbour; though you would never have known it was Sunday by the way they behaved. They drank out of their saucers and carried on in a very rude manner. So you see with all this custom I must really have to help in serving the teas, and

96

'I wonder whether you two creatures would care to do a little work for me?' inquired Mrs Goose (*page 96*)

A crowd of animals poured into the shop (*page 102*)

'Well, my little animal. And how are you to-day?' said the Mayor (*page 104*)

'I never thought it would be my painful duty to take the name and address of the Mayor of Toytown,' said Ernest (*page 111*)

if you would care to come here in the afternoons and assist me I should be willing to pay you a little pocket-money.'

'How much?' Dennis inquired.

'Well, say threepence each a week,' Mrs. Goose suggested.

'It is not enough,' replied Dennis. 'You see we should have to keep up a very smart appearance if we in your shop served.'

'Oh, yes, Mrs. Goose,' cried Larry. 'And also we should be so fearfully tempted; and I don't think we ought to be exposed to such dreadful temptation without being paid extra for it.'

'Temptation,' said Mrs. Goose. 'What kind of temptation?'

'Oh, Mrs. Goose, ma'am,' replied Larry. 'Think of all those lovely cakes and things, and how we should want to eat them! However should we be able to prevent ourselves from eating the stock on threepence a week!'

'It couldn't be done,' said Dennis. 'Not for less than six-pence a week.'

'Well, I would be willing to try you at sixpence a week each,' Mrs. Goose told them. 'But you will have to be very smart and polite, and you must never let me catch you eating cakes or sweets in my shop.'

'We'll see that never doing that us will you catch, ma'am.' Dennis replied. Then the two animals consulted together in whispers and at last announced that they were prepared to do their best. So Mrs. Goose took them behind the counter, gave each of them an apron, and began to explain everything to them.'

'I shall want you to serve the teas,' she said. 'I shall stand behind the counter, filling the tea-pots and all that, and you two animals must carry the things on these trays to the little tables where the customers sit. Now, my teas are sixpence each, and for that a customer gets a small pot of tea, a plate of bread and butter and cakes.'

'It's a lot of money,' remarked Dennis.

'Ah, but then, you see, a person is allowed as much as he can eat for that. If he wants more cakes he can have them.'

'Oh, Mrs. Goose, ma'am; then sixpence is cheap,' said Larry.

'Well, not really very cheap,' remarked Mrs. Goose, 'because, you see, a person can hardly eat sixpennyworth of cakes at a sitting.'

'He could standing up,' replied Dennis.

'Perhaps,' said Mrs. Goose, 'but people sit at the tables in this shop. People are expected to behave politely here. The only person who is allowed to take tea standing is Mr. Ernest; he drops in sometimes and prefers to take his tea at the counter where there is plenty of room for his elbows.'

'And can he eat more than sixpennyworth of cakes, ma'am?' Larry inquired.

'He never tries,' Mrs. Goose replied. 'Mr. Ernest is always quite the gentleman.'

Then the old lady left the two friends to tidy up the shop while she made some cakes. For some time they worked in silence and Larry observed that Dennis was very thoughtful: he kept pausing and scratching his ears, and then he would look at the things on the counter and do sums on his paws. At last Larry could bear it no longer. 'What are you thinking about, Dennis?' he asked.

'Cakes, my friend,' Dennis answered. 'I've got an idea.'

'Oh, but, Dennis, we promised we wouldn't eat the cakes,' Larry whispered.

'We didn't,' replied Dennis. 'We promised we wouldn't let Frau Goose us eating them catch.'

'I don't think it would be right for us to eat Mrs. Goose's cakes, for all that,' said Larry. 'Besides, she'd notice some had gone. But they're certainly an awful temptation, and I don't mind listening to your idea, Dennis.'

'Well, what I have been thinking, my friend, is this. Supposing a very big, fat man came into this shop for a sixpenny tea; and supposing he could eat much more than sixpennyworth of cakes. Supposing he kept on asking for more cakes, and supposing we served him with ever so many platefuls. That would be all right, wouldn't it?'

'Yes,' Larry agreed. 'That would be all right, because Mrs. Goose said that a customer could have as many cakes as he could eat.'

Dennis leaned forward and dug his friend in the ribs with his paw. 'But where he must eat them she did not say, was it?' he said with a chuckle. 'Listen, my friend, to you my great idea I will whisper.'

When Dennis had finished whispering, Larry looked rather nervous and uncomfortable. 'It doesn't seem quite right to me,' he said, 'but it's a splendid idea. I should never have thought of it. And it's a dreadful temptation, because if we did it we should have all the cakes we wanted to eat for weeks.'

'Then how about it, was it?' asked Dennis.

'Well, you see, Dennis, I'm afraid my little conscience won't let me help,' replied Larry.

'Ha, you are afraid, you are afraid,' cried Dennis, 'so to help me be a waiter you had better not.'

'I'm not afraid,' said Larry. 'Only a little timid. All lambs are timid. But I don't really think I had better be a waiter with you, after all. You see, it's not only my little conscience; it's Ernest the policeman as well. He might catch me. He's very clever and I'm sure he's suspicious of us already.'

'Care not for Ernest, my friend. Never will he suspect; never, never, never.'

'And there's another reason as well as Ernest and my little conscience why I ought not to be a waiter,' Larry continued. 'You see, I'm really supposed to be looking after Letitia.'

'Letitia!' cried Dennis. 'What was this Letitia?'

'Letitia is a little girl lamb,' Larry explained. 'A very little

99

lamb indeed; only a lambkin. She's so small she can't talk very
well yet, and I promised Farmer Giles I would not let her get
into mischief. And I don't think I ought to be a bad example for
her.'

'Very well, my friend. Go; go; your little conscience with you
also. And perhaps it is that you would not for me a little
message take, was it?'

'What message?' asked Larry, suspiciously.

'To the pig and baby elephant of Mr. Noah I would ask you
to go, into their ears quietly whispering: "The clever Dennis,"
you will say, "behind the back door of Frau Goose's shop
awaits you, there great things to discuss. As many friends as
you like bring with you also, particularly those who from
hunger suffer." '

'Very well, I don't mind doing that,' Larry agreed. 'But if
any one asks me what it's all about, I shall say I don't know
anything.'

'Very good, my friend, you know nothing; it is understood,
Now go, and leave me here my duties to perform.'

So Larry nervously hurried from the shop, leaving Dennis
tidying the tables and counting the cream buns.

★ ★ ★ ★ ★

Some days later Ernest the policeman was passing Mrs.
Goose's shop. He stopped to look at the tempting array of cakes
in the window and saw through the glass the figure of Dennis
the dachshund, wearing an apron, and hurrying about between
the tables and the counter with a little round tray. Without
hesitation Ernest stepped into the shop. Dennis saw him at
once and saluted jauntily with his paw.

'Good day, constable,' he said. 'It was a lovely day, was it?
Will you this table take? All to yourself you can have it because
some friends of mine have just gone.' And he began wiping the
top of the table with a cloth. 'Good-afternoon to you, my lad,'
said Ernest. 'So friends of yours have been sitting here, have

they?'

'Yes, it was so, officer,' replied Dennis. 'Tea they have been having.'

'Having tea, were they? Looks to me as if they were having a bath. Don't you go a-swishing that spilt milk on to my new trousers; I've got on a new uniform, I have.'

'And very smart you look, officer, on this fine afternoon,' remarked Dennis. 'Was it one of our sixpenny teas you would like?'

'No, my lad, it wasn't,' Ernest replied. 'I'm a-going to have a nice cup o' tea at the counter with Mrs. Goose. None of your polite teas for me. What are you a-doing here, may I ask?'

'Waiting,' replied Dennis.

'Waiting? What for?'

'Sixpence a week, officer.'

'Oh, you mean being a waiter?' said Ernest. 'Well, you mind your p's and q's, my lad; I've had my eye on you for some time.' And, moving to the counter, he saluted Mrs. Goose, who giggled and then poured out some tea into a large breakfast-cup which she kept especially for Ernest.

'It's a lovely day, officer,' said Mrs. Goose.

'You never spoke a truer word than that, ma'am.' replied Ernest. 'It is a lovely day: I told the Mayor so only this morning. But to change the subject, ma'am, I see you've got that long sausage dog here. May I ask how you came to take him on? I thought he was a turn-spit by trade.'

'He was a turn-spit,' Mrs. Goose agreed, 'but he found it made his front legs so bandy, turning the wheel round; and the dear creature is so sensitive. He thought if he did a little running about and waiting in my shop it would exercise his back legs for a change.'

'Oh, he did, did he, ma'am?' said Ernest. 'Well, you keep your eye on him. I know a thing or two about that young fellow. As an officer of the law it ain't for me to go saying things what I can't prove, but I see no harm in mentioning that the law regards him with very grave suspicion. Watch him ma'am'.

'Oh, I'm sure you must be mistaken, officer,' Mrs. Goose replied. 'He is a most conscientious dog and very interested in the business. Do you know he has gone to a lot of trouble to get his friends to come here for tea? Quite a crowd of them was here yesterday having our sixpenny teas.'

'And ate you out of house and home, I'll be bound,' remarked Ernest. 'Do I understand that a person taking a sixpenny tea can have all the cakes he can eat?'

'Certainly,' Mrs. Goose replied. 'And I must admit that after those animals had gone I had to set to and bake a fresh lot of cakes for next day. They didn't leave a cake in the place; but perhaps the poor dears were hungry.'

'Perhaps they were, poor little darlings,' said Ernest. 'Well, I must be going, ma'am, having my duties to perform, as you might say. Thank you for the tea; you certainly can make tea, ma'am. I always say to everyone, you can say what you like about Mrs. Goose, but she can make a nice cup o' tea.'

Soon after the policeman's departure the door swung open and a crowd of animals poured into the shop and seated themselves at the tables. There was Toby a nice dog from Farmer Giles', a baby elephant carrying a school satchel, a nearly fully grown kangaroo, two young bears wearing sailor-suits, a very gross looking pig with an attache case, and a baby hippo carrying a sack which looked like hay. They each ordered a sixpenny tea and Dennis hastened to serve them. But Mrs. Goose sighed, for she recognised the animals as friends of Dennis and hoped they were not feeling so hungry on this occasion. But she had no time to watch them, for, just then, the door again opened and in came the Mayor of Toytown carrying a hand-trunk and followed by Larry the lamb. Mrs. Goose left the counter and hurried towards the Mayor.

'Good afternoon, Mrs. Goose,' said the Mayor. 'I am going to

102

pick up a coach for Arkville, and as I have some time to spare I thought I would drop into your excellent establishment and take one of your famous sixpenny teas. This Larry very kindly offered to carry my bag so I have brought him in to have tea as a treat.'

'I am sure my shop is greatly honoured, your worship', replied Mrs. Goose. 'Will you take this table?'

'I think I should prefer the one over there,' replied the Mayor. 'A little further away from that pig. His manners are, ahem, not quite what we are accustomed to at the Town Hall. But I suppose you get all sorts of people in here, Mrs. Goose? Well, now, I understand that a person partaking of a sixpenny tea is allowed plenty of cakes. I am extremely partial to cakes. I will have one of your sixpenny teas. And would you like a sixpenny tea, my lamb?'

'Oh, Mr. Mayor, sir,' replied Larry, 'it was very kind of you to bring me in here for tea, but I don't drink tea. It's bad for my little nerves. If you don't mind I'll have a glass of milk and a cream bun.'

'Certainly, my lamb; certainly,' said the Mayor.

'And, please, Mrs. Goose, will you cut my cream bun into quarters?' Larry added. 'Because I find that when I try to bite a whole cream bun it always squirts; and as I am having tea with the Mayor I want to be polite.'

'A very proper spirit,' said the Mayor. 'Very proper. I am glad to know you were so well brought up. I wish I could say as much for those animals over there. I hope they are not friends of yours?'

'Oh, no, Mr. Mayor, sir,' Larry replied. 'They're friends of Dennis, and very rough. I never play with them because I'm such a little lamb, and the elephant and the hippo are very big; if I played with them I might get squashed.'

'Quite right, my lamb. A rough elephant is not a suitable playmate for a young lamb. Ah, here is the tea, and plenty of

103

cakes, I perceive. Plenty of cakes.'

But just as the Mayor was reaching for his first cake the door opened a few inches and in peeped a very small baby lamb.

'I seed you!' cried the baby lamb.

'Why, whatever is that?' exclaimed the Mayor.

'Oh, Mr. Mayor, sir, please don't look,' said Larry. 'Then perhaps she'll go away. It's a little girl lamb, and Farmer Giles asked me to keep her out of mischief. I bought her a toffee-apple on a stick for a halfpenny, but she knows I have three-halfpence of my pocket-money left and she keeps on following me about. That's the worst of girls.'

'Lawy!' cried the baby lamb. 'I seed you; I seed you.'

'Oh, Mr. Mayor, sir; I'm afraid she won't go away,' said Larry. 'Would you mind if she had tea with us?'

'Well, of course, when I asked you to tea I hardly expected to have to entertain half the animals of Toytown as well,' replied the Mayor. 'However, perhaps you had better ask her in.'

But the baby lamb did not wait to be invited. She scampered up to the table and began tugging at Larry's fleece. 'Hullo,' she said. 'I seed you!'

'Well, my little animal. And how are you to-day?' said the Mayor.

'I isn't a ickle animal. I's a ickle lamb,' replied the baby lamb.

'And what is your name, my little lamb?' the Mayor asked.

''Titia,' answered the baby lamb.

'Your little playmate appears to have caught a cold,' the Mayor remarked to Larry.

'Oh, no, Mr. Mayor, sir,' said Larry. 'She hasn't. That was not a sneeze; she was trying to tell you her name. It's Letitia; but she can't talk properly because she's so small.'

'Ah, quite, quite. Well now, Letitia, what would you like for your tea?'

'Stickums,' replied Letitia.

104

'Oh, Mr. Mayor, sir, don't let her,' cried Larry. 'She means a toffee-apple on a stick, and she's had one already. And look at her; her wool's all sticky. I think she had better have a banana.'

'Nana! Nana!' cried Letitia enthusiastically.

'Would you mind lending me your pocket-handkerchief, Mr. Mayor, sir?' Larry asked. 'She is supposed to wear a bib, but a handkerchief tied round here neck would do.'

'Well, really——!' began the Mayor. But he lent his hand-kerchief, after some hesitation, and Larry tied it round the neck of his young friend. Then Dennis arrived with the banana on a very large plate, and the Mayor had to peel it, Larry being unable to do so on account of his hoofs. The baby lamb then became very busy.

When the Mayor and Larry had finished their tea the Mayor paid Mrs. Goose, complimented her on the excellence of her cakes and left the shop with his bag, followed by Larry. But outside he stopped and looked at his watch.

'Dear, dear,' said the Mayor, 'I have still fifteen minutes to wait. I should be grateful, my lamb, if you would remain here with my bag while I hurry to the police station for a word with the constable. I shall just have time.'

The Mayor walked quickly away, leaving Larry standing upon the curb, the Mayor's large bag beside him. The Mayor had hardly turned the corner when the animal-friends of Dennis came trooping from the shop, their bags and satchels over their shoulders; and Larry observed that the bags and satchels looked very much heavier than they had done before. The animals passed round behind the shop and just then Ernest the policeman came hurrying back, breathing hard.

'May I ask whose bag that is, my lad?' he asked.

'Oh, yes, Mr. Ernest, sir, you may,' replied Larry. 'It's the Mayor's bag. I am waiting here for him because he's just gone to the police-station to look for you.'

'Looking for me, is he?' said Ernest. 'Well, I'm afraid he's

105

a-wasting of his time. I've got to have a word with Mrs. Goose, I have. Didn't I see a crowd of low animals a-trooping into this shop just as I was a-leaving? All carrying bags, and sacks and what not?'

'Oh, yes, Mr. Ernest, sir, I expect you did.'

'Ah, I thought so. I thought my eyes had not deceived me. And I've just thought of something. I must speak to Mrs. Goose at once.'

Ernest hurried into the shop, leaving Larry looking very nervous and uncomfortable upon the pavement. But Larry did not remain there; he crept to the door of the shop on the tips of his little hoofs and put his ear to the crack. As he listened Larry began to tremble and then, picking up the Mayor's bag, he ran off in the direction taken by the friends of Dennis the dachshund.

*　　　*　　　*　　　*　　　*

Mrs. Goose was standing in her shop looking sadly at the empty counter.

'Well I never!' she cried. 'Not a cake left; not one!'

'To-morrow some more we shall want,' said Dennis. 'Never any one who ate so many cakes as the Mayor have I seen. Never.'

'The Mayor!' exclaimed Mrs. Goose. 'Do you mean to say his worship the Mayor ate all those cakes!'

'He must, he must, Frau Goose. Because to my friends I said: 'Do not be greedy now, just because a lot of cakes you are allowed. Of Frau Goose's good nature do not advantage take. And they did not advantage take; particularly I noticed it.'

'Well, I am surprised!' said Mrs. Goose. 'I should never have thought the Mayor would have been so greedy.'

'Ah, with these fat people you cannot tell, you cannot tell. Particularly when they have eyes which goggle.' replied Dennis.

106

Just then Ernest the policeman came hurrying into the shop.

'Mrs. Goose, ma'am, Mrs. Goose,' he cried, breathlessly, 'I've been thinking.'

'The good officer has been thinking,' said Dennis. 'To tell us so he comes. It was unusual, was it not?'

'Don't you go being sarcastic, my lad. I've spoke to you before about being sarcastic. Mrs. Goose, Ma'am, when I was going back to my beat after that nice cup o' tea you were kind enough to give me, I started thinking about what you said regarding all your cakes disappearing. I was a-turning it over in my mind, as you might say. And then I remembered I'd seen a crowd of low animals go into your shop with bags and all, and it all come over me in a flash.'

'A flash, officer!' cried Mrs. Goose.

'Yes, ma'am, I see it all,' said Ernest. 'You're the victim of a plot. All those low animals, not content with eating as many cakes as they can stuff into themselves, have been taking cakes away. Else why should they be carrying bags, and satchels, and trunks and what not?'

'Oh, surely not, officer,' Mrs. Goose cried. 'Why, those animals were friends of Dennis.'

'All the more reason why we should regard them with very grave suspicion, ma'am.'

'You was rude, officer, you was rude,' said Dennis. 'Always I myself respectable have kept.'

'Well, whether you're respectable, or whether you're not,' Ernest replied, 'I'm going to follow up your friends and search their bags and what not.'

Just then the shop-door swung open and in stumped Mr. Growser.

'I want some tea, I want some tea,' he cried. 'This is a tea-shop, is it not?'

'Yes, Mr. Growser, this is a tea-shop,' Mrs. Goose replied with dignity. 'Or rather, it was a tea-shop.'

107

'Also a confectioner's it was,' Dennis added.

'What do you mean, ma'am?' Mr. Growser asked. 'Was a tea-shop, indeed! If it is a tea-shop you need not be ashamed to admit it. Either it is a tea-shop or it isn't. Now, madam, kindly pull yourself together and answer a plain question. Is this, or is this not a tea-shop?'

Dennis replied. 'Once a tea-shop this was where for sixpence large teas with many cakes one could obtain. But now was it not · that all stock has been eaten or away carried, therefore is it no longer a tea-shop, was it?'

'It is exactly as the dog says, Mr. Growser,' Mrs. Goose added.

'And what may that be, madam, what may that be? I haven't understood a word he has said. You ought to be ashamed to employ a waiter who is unable to make himself understood. I like plain English, madam—plain English!'

'I must ask you to speak more respectfully before a lady, Mr. Growser, sir,' Ernest interrupted. 'And to save further unpleasantness I may say that this is a tea-shop, and a very good tea-shop too. Famous for its sixpenny teas.'

'Very good, officer. Then why do they endeavour to conceal the fact? Why make a hole and corner business of it? I will have a sixpenny tea.'

'Well, of course, Mr. Growser, we always try to give satisfaction,' said Mrs. Goose, 'but on this occasion I'm afraid we can't give you a sixpenny tea. We've run out of sixpenny teas.'

'No more sixpenny teas have we,' cried Dennis. 'So famous the sixpenny tea, so great the rush, was it? Never, never, never.'

'This is disgraceful, disgraceful!' Mr. Growser shouted, thumping the floor with his umbrella. 'I wonder you can look me in the face. You offer me a sixpenny tea and when I ask for one you say you haven't any. It ought not to be allowed!'

'The fact of the matter is, Mr. Growser, that Mrs. Goose has been the subject of a deep-laid plot,' Ernest explained. 'Some one, I will mention no names, but some one has not only ate all the cakes they could for sixpence but has been and took cakes away.'

'Well, if they've eaten the cakes, of course they've taken them away,' cried Mr. Growser. 'Talk sense, officer; talk sense.'

'What I mean to say is that the cakes taken away was done so in a receptacle: in other words a bag, sack, or satchel or what not.'

'Then they ought to be ashamed of themselves!' cried Mr. Growser.

'They ought,' Ernest agreed. 'But I will ask you kindly to stop thumping with your umbrella like that, Mr. Growser, sir. You're making Mrs. Goose's crockery rattle and shake something shocking.'

'Nonsense, nonsense. That's the stage-coach,' Mr. Growser replied. 'It has just stopped outside. Look for yourself, officer: look for yourself.' And Mr. Growser pointed at the window.

'Ha!' he continued, 'and if you knew your duties, constable, you would perceive a fat, overfed person and a large bag. And if you had any intelligence you would put two and two together.'

'Here, what's all this?' cried Ernest. And he dashed from the shop followed by Mr. Growser, Mrs. Goose, and Dennis.

The coach had stopped just outside the shop, the Mayor was just preparing to enter it; Larry the lamb was standing near and looking rather uncomfortable, and the driver was pulling the Mayor's large bag up toward the roof.

On catching sight of Ernest, Larry uttered a loud and frightened 'Baah!' which so startled the driver that he let the bag slip from his hands. It fell to the pavement and burst open, and out poured cakes, cream buns, plain buns, rock-cakes and every other kind of cake.'

'Well, I never!' cried Ernest.

109

'You ought to be ashamed of yourself!' shouted Mr. Growser. 'The Mayor of Toytown, setting an example like this!'

'Oh, Mr. Mayor, sir, I never thought you were so greedy!' said Larry the lamb.

'Why, but this is a most extraordinary thing!' exclaimed the Mayor. 'That is my bag, is it not?'

'Of course it's your bag, sir!' shouted Mr. Growser. 'Hasn't it a large 'T' painted on it? T stands for Toytown, sir, does it not? It also stands for Thief!'

'How dare you make such a suggestion, Mr. Growser!' cried the Mayor. 'Do you imply that I have stolen these buns?'

'Have you, or have you not had a sixpenny tea?' Mr. Growser asked.

110

'I certainly have partaken of a sixpenny tea,' the Mayor admitted.

Mr. Growser thumped the pavement with his umbrella. 'And what you couldn't eat, sir, you stuffed into your bag. And we find you taking your ill-gotten gains away in the coach. I wonder you could look the horses in the face!'

'I never thought it would be my painful duty to take the name and address of the Mayor of Toytown——' began Ernest.

'You are being absurd, officer; absurd,' said the Mayor. 'This is a ridiculous mistake. I should not dream of taking Mrs. Goose's cakes, except, of course, at the tea-table in a proper manner. And as for filling a bag with them——!'

'I seed you!' cried a piping voice. And the small figure of Letitia pushed between Ernest and Mr. Growser and sidled up to Larry, sucking one front hoof.

'Ha!' said Mr. Growser. 'Here is an animal who actually saw you in the act, sir; saw you in the act! It says so. Disgraceful!'

'This seems to be a very important witness,' remarked Ernest. 'What is your name, my lambkin?'

''Titia,' replied the baby lamb.

'Oh, Mr. Ernest, sir,' cried Larry. 'I don't think this little girl lamb means that she saw the mayor fill his bag with cakes. I think she just meant that she could see me.'

'I seed you,' said Letitia.

'She's been following me about all day because she knows I have three-halfpence,' Larry continued. 'That's worst of girls.'

'Now, tell me, lambkin,' said the Mayor. 'Did you see me fill a bag with cakes?'

'No, not 'oo,' replied Letitia.

'There, officer. You see I am perfectly innocent. This young lamb did not see me appropriating the cakes.'

'Ha, that's very important evidence, your worship,' remarked Ernest.

'Nothing of the sort! Nothing of the sort!' cried Mr.

111

Growser. 'The animal might not have been looking at the time. After all, there must be quite a lot of people in Toytown who did not see the cakes appropriated because they were not looking.'

'True, Mr. Growser; I never thought of that,' replied Ernest. 'Now, my lambkin, tell Uncle Ernest. Did you see anyone at all a-messing about with cakes or buns or such?'

'Ess.'

'Ha! And where did you see it? Speak up; don't be afraid.'

'Ahind Old Goosey's shop.'

'If you are referring to Mrs. Goose, my young lambkin. I must ask you to speak more respectful,' said Ernest. 'Now then, who or what did you see behind Mrs. Goose's shop?'

'A lot of amals. A piggy-wiggy, and a ickle white woofer, and a prolophant——'

'A whater?' asked Ernest.

'Oh, Mr. Ernest, sir; she means an elephant,' Larry explained. 'But she's such a very little lambkin that she can't talk very well.'

'Do you mean an elephant?' Ernest asked.'

'Ess. A eflant. And a woofer, and a big, big amal with a pocket in his fur——'

'Ha, a kangaroo!' exclaimed Ernest. 'And what were these creatures a-doing of?'

'They all had hundeds and hundeds and hundeds of buns. In bags. And the amal with a pocket in his fur had some in his pocket.'

'Ha, I suspected as much!' cried Ernest. 'So it was those low friends of Dennis after all. But what I want to know is: How did the buns get into the bag of his worship the Mayor of Toytown? Who did it?'

'Lawy,' said Letitia. 'I seed him.'

'Why, yes; he did mind my bag for me!' exclaimed the Mayor.

112

'To own up you had better, my friend,' said Dennis. 'Ah, my friend, how often have I not against girls warned you! And see what has happened, was it? A toffee-apple you buy her and away she gives you. It was sad, was it? Come, my friend, let us go.'

'Here, not so fast, my lad,' cried Ernest. 'Don't you go a-hurrying off like that. I want to know a little more about this first. What made you put the buns in the Mayor's bag?'

'It was his idea of a joke,' shouted Mr. Growser. 'I've noticed before that a lamb always has a curious sense of humour. It ought not to be allowed.'

'With the criminals he was glove in hand,' said Dennis. 'Often to him I have said: "Larry, my friend——" '

'I seed him,' said Letitia.

'Oh, Mr. Ernest and Mr. Mayor, sir,' cried Larry. 'I'm very sorry, but I meant well. I was only doing my little best for the animals because they were friends of Dennis. You see, I knew they had filled their bags with Mrs. Goose's cakes, and when I heard Mr. Ernest say he was suspicious and was going to search the bags of the animals, I got frightened. Because, you see, I thought it would be a dreadful scandal in Toytown, and I knew Dennis would never hold up his head again if the friends he had recommended to Mrs. Goose had their names and addresses taken for filling their bags with her cakes.'

'You was right, my friend; quite right. Ashamed I should have been. Ashamed.'

'So I thought I would save them. And I was minding the Mayor's bag, so I slipped after the animals, and told them Mr. Ernest was coming, and we filled the Mayor's bag with the cakes and then I ran back here with it. You see, I thought when I got the chance I would run into the shop and put the buns back on the counter, only the Mayor came back before I could do it.'

'The whole business was most unfortunate,' said the Mayor.

113

'Most unfortunate. Though I feel compelled to admit that the lamb acted with a good motive. Loyalty to his friends. Ahem. Mistaken loyalty, but still——'

'It seems to me more like obstructing the law in the execution of its duty, your worship,' observed Ernest.

'Well, perhaps, officer. Perhaps. However, in the circumstances, I feel we may allow the matter to rest so far as Larry is concerned.'

'Very well, your worship, if you say so,' said Ernest. 'You being the party what has suffered most. As for me, I'm a-going to have a talk with those low, thieving animals, I am.'

'I will never have those greedy creatures in my shop again!' cried Mrs. Goose.

'Ah, Frau Goose,' said Dennis, sadly shaking his head. 'Never for having introduced them will I myself forgive. Never, never. And to be a waiter for you again I shall be too ashamed. I ask you for my sixpence, therefore, which to me you promised. Then I will go away with my friend Larry. But before I go shall I this last sad duty perform of picking up these cakes and buns, to dust them and upon the counter of your establishment to neatly replace them?'

'Oh, no, Dennis,' replied Mrs. Goose. 'I cannot serve my customers with soiled buns.'

'Ah, I feared so, I feared so. Then, Larry, my friend, let us these cakes and buns remove from in front of the excellent establishment of Frau Goose. Let us take them and of them dispose.'

'Oh, Dennis, all right,' said Larry. 'I'll help you to take them away.'

'Lawy, Lawy,' cried Letitia. 'I'll come wiv you. I like buns too.'

A Biographical
Note About the Author

ABOUT 1920, a man could be met striding along the Golders Green Road in north-west London and although he was carrying under his arm a large folder used by artists, he was dressed to give the impression that his work embraced nothing beyond that of a manager of a bank or a cautious solicitor. He was tall and thin with a clear-cut profile, and was carefully attired in black coat and waistcoat, cravat, striped trousers and a trilby hat.

Sydney George Hulme Beaman was born in Tottenham, London, on the twenty-eighth day of February, 1887, and with his two younger sisters he belonged to a professional family sometimes achieving fame or fortune in the time of Queen Victoria. He was the great-grandson of George Beaman, MD, FRCS, who was the founder of the New Equitable Life Assurance Company with Dr Thomas Wakeley, who established the chief journal of the English medical profession, *The Lancet*, in 1823. His grandfather was also a surgeon, his father was an insurance surveyor, and his mother ran away from home to become a singer and actress with the stage name of Nellie Leslie. As a boy he received a reasonable education, was prepared to study his books and was clever with his hands. Anything mechanical aroused his interest. The description would fit the average intelligent boy of his time, and perhaps the circumstance of his birth, coupled with indifferent health, were the factors which determined his future career.

Probably he inherited his love of the theatre from his mother, and visits to the annual pantomime coloured his imagination with the Harlequinade and transformation scene, at its best in the Victorian theatre. She moved in the London theatrical circle and spoke with affection about Lillie Langtry, the actress, and Charles Hawtrey, the actor-manager who was also a gifted comedian. On her birthday in 1893, Henry Irving gave her the cockade he had worn when playing Dubosc in *The Lyons Mail*.

There were writers in the family with Emeric Hulme Beaman, the

115

novelist, who was blind; Ardern George Hulme Beaman, author and journalist with Reuters in London's Fleet Street; Sir Frank Clement Offley Beaman, judge of the Indian Court, also philosophical writer; and Ardern Arthur Hulme Beaman, author and High Sheriff of Gloucestershire, 1948. No doubt the boy joined in conversation which kindled his wit, and from his father he may have received the integrity of purpose with the care and attention to the smallest detail evident in his later work.

His schooling was completed and he had little to unlearn of strange ideas or formal education to one of the professions. He decided to become an artist against the wish of his father, who preferred his son to follow the more stable vocation of architect. His mother, however, resolved the family difference of opinion, and with her tender entreaty the young Hulme Beaman became a student at Heatherley's well-known art school founded in 1845, though it is clear from S. G. Hulme Beaman's illustrations to his books that in his training he managed to avoid the formal path of the studious artist. The original and unusual style of his work was retained throughout his career.

The music-hall was very influential about this time and Hulme Beaman, during his student days, formed an amateur group known as the Dickens Fellowship, and he adapted characters created by Charles Dickens for recitation. He acted such parts as Fagin, Uriah Heep and Mr Peggotty and received invitations to perform professionally at smoking concerts which were as popular in the Edwardian era as music-halls. He met his wife Maud Mary Poltock through his stage performances, and she continued to play the musical accompaniment to his recital at the piano.

The decline of the music-hall and smoking concerts coincided with the end of the 1914-18 war, and Hulme Beaman turned to Noah's Ark and the Victorian wooden animals it contained. He started to make toys for which there was a demand since German toys had vanished from the shelves of the toyshops, and he set up his studio in a room on the first floor of a rented house in Golders Green. Here were installed a work-bench, drawing-board with watercolour paints, paint spray, Hobbies treadle fretwork saw, carpenter's tools and a gas burner for heating over a tripod a pot of gum arabic. There was a comfortable warmth about the place with the smell of wood shavings, pigments, varnish and the all-pervading odour of resin glue always on the boil to keep it liquid.

After carving the toy animals, Hulme Beaman considered Mr Noah and his wife, and these adult figures provided him with the idea from which his TOYTOWN characters, stories and illustrations later emerged. Once the human characterization was mastered and drawn, he carved the small

116

angular wooden figures about 4 in tall, with the treadle fretwork saw, and over the years there flowed an almost endless variety of unique humorous figures carved by his hand from his fertile brain. A ship was made with the crew carved and painted in authentic period style to line the deck of a Jolly Roger which was carefully researched. Topgallant, sprit-sail and 'bonnet' were scaled to rigging with miniature blocks, and a small brass cannon was lathe-turned. The ship was painted in appropriate colours; it floated, and was purchased for £5 by Heals, the London store. Other commissions followed, and soon there were brightly coloured jousting knights in armour carved to hold lances with their horses, and strange green demonic figures stood on square-toed legs which, with their arms and head, could be moved in various ways. A mounted highwayman with mask and pistol held up the stage coach, a stylized replica of the Georgian vehicle with two fine horses, a driver with his whip and an armed guard seated on the box at the rear of the coach.

Hulme Beaman's toys caught the fancy of young people around the district of north-west London, for they were unlike anything provided for children at that time. His whimsical ideas embodied in the square wooden figures attracted the attention of the London Press: 'Mr Beaman invented a new wonderland, not inhabited by fairies, but by very solid beings carved out of blocks of wood, and it says much for their inventor's genius that these quaint wooden figures have more vitality than many of the 'real' people one reads about in books.' Ceaselessly creative, he designed colourful humorous figures derived from every period in history. Egyptian characters jostled with Elizabethan and Georgian figures, and a caricature of a tall, thin Sherlock Holmes gazed perceptively at a figure he called 'The Old Witch', which bore an undeniable likeness to his mother-in-law.

The popularity of his work continued, and the world of toys peopled by 'little folk' from time immemorial encouraged the demand for his ideas. Near his studio was a riding school called Kimbolton Lodge which contained a small stabled outbuilding overlooking a paddock where the horses were exercised. Hulme Beaman recruited two friends and instructed them in his method of carving with the treadle fretwork machine. Attached to an oak tree was a painted sign of a square, portly man wearing a white apron with his cleaver firmly implanted in a butcher's wooden carving stool and inscribed with the words: 'Hulme Beaman Toys Are Made Here—Bring the Kiddies'.

Golders Green in the nineteen-twenties was growing, and, situated near to the Hampstead Garden Suburb, was a favourite with artists, writers and actors. Hulme Beaman had a community of friends, and among them was

Dando (a well-known name with circus folk) who invented the Flying Ballet. While court jester to the mad King Ludwig of Bavaria, he had an act where he shot his wife from a cannon. He was a little man with flowing white hair and wore a broad-brimmed black hat, red lined cloak with a metal clasp and high-heeled boots. There was Ambrose Manning, a rather plump actor who had an important part in *The Farmer's Wife* by Eden Phillpotts, and Frank Cochrane, who played and sang the part of the beggar in the musical play *Chu-Chin-Chow* throughout a long run at Her Majesty's Theatre.

The creation of the small figures was a means of existence. They were sold as toys for the amusement of youngsters, and provided a modest livelihood for the artist designing them. Nevertheless, Hulme Beaman was an actor, and therefore an entertainer who, unconsciously perhaps, was assembling in his mind the cast for a performance which was awaiting production in a theatrical form. He was also a story-teller who endeavoured to escape from the conflict of everyday existence into the world of make-believe for his own and our pleasure. Pictures communicate ideas and although the 'still' picture illustrates an event crystallized for all time, there is another form of picture-making whereby the drawings illustrate in continuity a sequence of events. The cartoon drawing not only describes a story but each picture directs attention to the next episode. The method has an important asset—the humour or sense of the ridiculous—that no 'still' picture can convey.

The cartoon illustration is derived from the allegorical drawing which has a hidden meaning as well as the one first observed when it is viewed. In Italy the sixteenth century painter Annibale Carracci was the first artist to amuse himself and his friends by making caricatures or comic pictures of living people and several artists followed his example. A drawing by James Gillray made fun of an eighteenth century fashion for plumes when he drew a sedan chair carrying a lady with an enormous plumed headpiece protruding through the roof of the sedan chair, carried by two hapless retainers. Hulme Beaman observed the caricature humour of this incident when he included a sedan chair carried by two redoubtable stalwarts among his TOYTOWN figures.

Newspapers promoted the strip cartoon for children, where the story is illustrated with a series of little pictures, and these gave Hulme Beaman the opportunity to develop his art. *The Golders Green Gazette* was a small suburban newspaper which offered him space for his drawings and story-line. He created a series entitled 'Philip and Phido', which first saw the light of day when it was published as a weekly feature on the 30 November, 1923, and specimens of which follow on the next three pages.

118

Philip and Phido set out

They meet a highwayman

A greeting from the Admiral

They are picked up by the Martian Fuz

They fight the dreaded Wiggly-wog

But return to earth and go to the circus
(*note Ernest the policeman and other characters who reappear in Toytown*)

The adventures of a boy and his dog began on the road to Dover. Hulme Beaman's method was to carve the wooden figures and then illustrate what he saw to accompany the cartoon captions: 'When people set out to seek their fortunes,' said Philip, 'they always take a bundle on a stick with them. I have a clean collar and some bread in mine; what have you in your bundle, Phido?' 'I have my best brass collar and a juicy bone,' replied Phido; 'but the bone won't be in my bundle much longer. I'm hungry.' Meeting a highwayman about to hold up the stage coach, they captured him and were rewarded with a voyage on a ship sailing to the Spanish Main. They were enlisted by the Admiral on the ship, and in the 'Toytown' stories written later, the character of the Mayor of Toytown was derived from the Admiral, stout and important who for all that thought he was 'a fine figure of a man'.

Adventures continued swiftly, and their encounter with the Wiggly-Wog was followed by the dreaded Martian Fuz, something between a dragon and a bird, who plucked them into the sky to drop them to the top of a mountain and through the mouth of a volcano into a dark pit. All was not lost, and Philip and Phido were surprised (as was everyone else) to find themselves in the mountain workshop of Father Christmas. The old gentleman, blessed with modern invention, had his sleigh fitted with an aeroplane propeller. Even a magic sledge has to be well oiled, and this was done thoroughly before Philip and Phido clambered up behind the boxes of presents which they helped Father Christmas to distribute to his young friends on their return to earth. Afterwards they were invited to join the grand parade of a circus travelling through the streets of the town … 'and when they all got back to the circus tent, they found a large crowd of people waiting to go in'. Marshalling the 'crowd' was Ernest the Policeman and in the queue was Mr Growser, wearing a beard, and Peter Brass carrying an umbrella, who would be making a name for themselves later in the TOYTOWN stories.

The publication of his cartoon series in the local newspaper, with his inventive figures and toys, brought a constant stream of young visitors to Hulme Beaman's workshop at Kimbolton Lodge who wanted to find out how all this was done. There was interest too from schools, and the Woodstock School, Golders Green, arranged with him to conduct a Toymaking and Woodworking class for the benefit of the school's pupils. The 'wireless' became an absorbing hobby at this time with the daily programme of the BBC. 'Listening-in' to the early broadcasts with the aid of headphones encouraged youngsters to make their own crystal set with the fine wire known as the 'cat's whisker', carefully selecting the spot on the crystal for receiving the best signal. Hulme Beaman, unaware of the important part the BBC was to play in his career, assembled his own radio set and conducted a Wireless Class on how to do it with a cigar-box, galena crystal, cat's whisker and the tuning coil connected to the aerial.

His creative work continued in the time that remained from guiding the young in their new activity. *Aladdin* retold and illustrated by Hulme Beaman was a decorative and entertaining children's full-length book and was published in 1924 by John Lane, The Bodley Head. This was followed by A Series of Illustrated Tales for Children with the titles of four short stories published by the Oxford University Press in 1925. The first story was *The Road to Toytown**, and it described Tom and his dog Trot as they rode on a magic broomstick to arrive in Toytown, where they were entertained by Harlequin and the other novel people they discovered there. It contained the Hulme Beaman drawings of the quaint Toytown houses that became the theatrical background of all the subsequent Toytown illustrations and was republished in a volume of ten short stories called *Stories from Toytown* by the Oxford University Press in 1938. Another adaptation of a children's classic story was *The Seven Voyages of Sinbad the Sailor* which appeared in 1926, published by John Lane, and the story he retold was illustrated in his unique style of drawing. For younger children, Frederick Warne published the *Out of the Ark Books* in 1927 which Hulme Beaman illustrated with a brief story line and they were also translated and published in France.

'The Tale of the Magician' in which the following occurs was one of six stories in the volume entitled *Tales of Toytown* published by the Oxford University Press in 1928:

Number 2 Ark Street was a curious-looking house. It was built of grey stone with a steep roof, and had a very mysterious-looking doorway. The door was thick and heavy, and in the middle of it had been painted a mysterious magic sign. In this house lived the Magician; at least, everyone called him the Magician. He was really quite a nice old gentleman, but the people of Toytown felt rather frightened of him, and anyone passing down Ark Street after dark was always particular to walk on the opposite side of the road; though as the street was narrow the passer-by still had to walk close to the house. But it was as well to keep as far from the Magician's house as possible, and especially from the magic sign; for everyone knows that magicians think nothing of turning people into elephants or something equally uncomfortable when they happen to feel annoyed.

However, there was one person who was not afraid of the Magician's house, or of the Magician; in fact, he was not afraid of anything—or so he said. This was the Mayor of Toytown.

*With which this present collection opens.

His opening lines gave some indication of the wit and wry sense of humour expressed by Hulme Beaman in the tales that were never 'written down' for children for they were accepted as individuals in their own right. His characters were broadly defined with efficient memorable characterization as occurs in all popular classics, and he created a world that made their imaginary existence something more than merely funny.

The book was the turning-point in the author's progress, and through broadcasting his stories became favourites with millions of young (and also not so young) listeners to the BBC Children's Hour programmes. It attracted the attention of May Jenkin, 'Elizabeth' of the Children's Hour, as she described in the *Radio Times* in 1936:

> I happened upon a modest little book entitled 'Tales of Toytown'; the illustrations in particular struck me as extraordinarily attractive, and a perusal of the letterpress convinced us all that here was first-rate broadcast material. When the first six tales came to an end we wrote to the author demanding more. He came to see us, shyly delighted that his stories had pleased us, and three weeks later, with equal diffidence, he produced a further Toytown adventure. This was the beginning of an extraordinarily fruitful collaboration between Mr Hulme Beaman and the talented interpreters of his work. Every three or four weeks, over a period of two years, he sent us a new story . . . and to Mr Hulme Beaman belongs the rare achievement of having created some dozen characters which, to Children's Hour listeners, are nearly as well known as Alice and the White Rabbit were in my nursery—characters which are the very stuff of radio created for and by broadcasting.

Accustomed as he was to the discipline of the printed page, Hulme Beaman found no difficulty in adapting his episodes to the discipline of broadcasting in sound radio. Situation, characterization and dialogue were abundant in his imagination, and he came to understand the possibilities of the dialogue form of story-telling acceptable to the BBC Children's Hour radio programme. Although most of the main Toytown characters he created in the six stories of *Tales of Toytown*, the animal characters of Larry the Lamb and Dennis the Dachshund were only briefly introduced. These two characters became more prominent in subsequent episodes, especially as Hulme Beaman realized he had an admirable interpreter of Larry in the Head of BBC Children's radio programmes: Derek McCulloch, and known to children everywhere as 'Uncle Mac.' He broadcast the parts of the Narrator and Larry the Lamb throughout the many years of the programme, arousing much affection from young viewers, and received many letters addressed to 'Larry the Lamb' at the Post Office.

Hulme Beaman said in modest words and another context that 'I shall do my best' and he continued to write the Children's Hour episodes. Nevertheless broadcasting to an unseen audience who were unable to see the 'extraordinarily attractive illustrations' mentioned by May Jenkin remained something he regarded as a challenge, and the discovery of the method whereby his characters were given visual life was delayed until later in his career.

For the time being, he returned to the theatrical side of his talent and made a model stage with proscenium and scenery in which he created a visual representation for string-controlled puppets of his story entitled *The Arkville Dragon**. There was a revolving stage enabling scenery to be set up before the performance started and at the appointed time the scene was revolved quickly into place for the curtain to rise. Above the velvet curtain with handsome gold tasselled border was the Toytown coat of arms supported by the Mayor of Toytown and Ernest the Policeman. The arms were quarterly, and pictured Mr Noah's ark, a Toytown house displaying a wireless aerial, the Inventor's saw with his glue-pot and some tintacks, and Dennis the Dachshund occupying a quarter on his own, with a crest above the shield depicting Larry the Lamb. On the sides of the proscenium arch, Hulme Beaman attached carved replicas of the traditional masks representing Comedy and Tragedy that occurred in early Greek plays. The small wooden marionettes were given extra weight with their feet cast in lead to keep them in contact with the stage.

The special event in the play was the Arkville Coach and horses with the Driver, Larry and Dennis seated on top as it travelled along the road through the forest from Toytown to the neighbouring town of Arkville. Not to be surpassed in theatrical effect, he painted a long panorama of the route which was mounted on rollers hidden from view. While the coach remained stationary with its wheels moving just above the stage and partly hidden by a scenic ground row, the background rolled merrily behind the coach with recorded music to complete the illusion. The toy theatre was called 'The Theatre Royal', and in a photograph taken after the performance, the BBC Aunts and Uncles (including Derek McCulloch) are grouped round the theatre with Beaman himself at his home in Golders Green: the men with wide trousers and brilliantined hair and girls with marcel waves of the nineteen-twenties.

He wrote twenty-eight episodes for the Children's Hour programme and re-wrote most of them for book publication. It is the book or literary form in

*Reprinted in this collection

which the stories appear in this volume, and the stories remain untouched, as do the characters.

In 1928, when Hulme Beaman's '*Tales of Toytown*' was published and he started his association with sound broadcasting, important progress occurred in the development of cartoon film animation and television. The first practical demonstration of colour television was given by John Logie Baird with a system using mechanical scanning of the subject and in that year he became the first person to transmit television across the Atlantic. On 19th September 1928 Walt Disney produced his 'Steamboat Willie', a cartoon film which incorporated sound and was an immediate success. It set the scene for drawn cartoon film animation over several years and Disney gave up drawing his own cartoons to become more of a film producer. Hulme Beaman observed the interest that the Disney cartoon films created and decided that his stories, illustrated as they were from figures he had carved, were more suitable for animation in the film three-dimensional puppet technique. However, it was not until four years later, in 1932, that his characters and ideas were put to the test of motion picture photography.

He obtained the assistance of the Pathé Film Company in Wardour Street, London, and they gave him studio space and camera to experiment in time-lapse photography with his characters. The filming was with the cumbersome equipment available at the time, and in the heat of the archaic studio lamps he developed with their technicians a film example of his work, carefully moving his carved wooden figures frame by frame for photography on the large 35mm cinema film then used. There was, of course, no colour, and the black and white representation of his Toytown houses and characters left something to be desired. He was encouraged with the result, and on the screen for the first time Neddy the donkey jumped through the window of a Toytown house and was met by Harlequin who seemed surprised to see it accomplished.

He wrote another episode for the Children's Hour programme and he succeeded with the idea to film his Toytown characters, though he died on 4th February. The following notice was published in a London newspaper:

Child listeners have lost a good friend. Mr. S. G. Hulme Beaman, the artist, actor and author, who died the other night from pneumonia, was so popular with the children because it was he who during the past three years had written the adventures that occur in Toytown. This was one of the best liked contributions to the Children's Hour. When preparing his broadcasts Mr. Beaman always worked out his ideas in a miniature theatre at his home. He would cut out in wood and paint all the characters and make them act as marionettes on the stage. As recently as Tuesday last he contributed to the Children's Hour. He will be greatly missed.

The British Broadcasting Company, as it was called, working from small studios in Savoy Hill, off the Strand, in London, became the largest broadcasting and television organisation in the world and generations of children—with grown-up eavesdroppers—were delighted with the Toytown stories. They were a constant repertory in the Children's Hour and the BBC rang the changes in the 28 stories always produced on Wednesdays. There were request weeks when children in homes throughout the country voted for their favourite programme and after twenty years of broadcasting, Toytown still led the way over new candidates.

From the most celebrated home in England came the request for a command performance and *The Disgraceful Business at Mrs Goose's** was the Toytown story performed in the presence of the Royal Family at Broadcasting House on the 13th. March, 1939.

New productions of the stories with local artists were broadcast in Australia and South Africa. The programme was recorded in the BBC Transcription service and eventually about two dozen territories in the Commonwealth obtained recordings of the series. A stage adaptation of *The Cruise of the Toytown Belle* was produced in London and a musical version of the Toytown stories. The EMI Company published long-playing recordings with artistes of the theatre play and 26 colour puppet films in time-lapse photography have been transmitted for television by the ITA Network in all regions. They are also distributed to several countries overseas.

It may be wondered what the modest author walking along the North End Road, Golders Green to seek inspiration for his stories on Hampstead Heath would think of the technical innovations over the last fifty years. Perhaps he would be content to know that the visual resources now provided are continuing the entertainment he invented and the characters created for new generations of children everywhere.

If a man write a better book, preach a better sermon, or make a better mousetrap than his neighbour, though he build his house in the woods, the world will make a beaten path to his door. — Ralph Waldo Emerson.

HENDRIK BAKER
July 1979

*Reprinted in this collection.